"Are you always this frank?"

Madison nodded. "It saves a lot of time."

Jack's lips curved suddenly, surprising her, and unleashing a mass of butterflies in her stomach. The smile reached his eyes and they actually seemed to change colour right before her, going from cool green to warm amber. "Okay, Hush it is."

"Yeah?" She smiled back, words deserting her. Unusual for her. But there was something about this man…

"But…" He held up his finger as if admonishing a naughty child. Even his hands were noteworthy. Tanned, with lean fingers and evenly clipped nails. No prissy manicure.

"I'm listening." Barely. Her stomach was just beginning to calm down.

"I still have veto power."

"Of course." Her gaze went again to his hands, to that perfect golden colour, so perfect it had to be artificial.

He squinted with suspicion. "What?"

"Are you tanned all over?"

Dear Reader,

By now you are probably as familiar with Hush as I am. After all, you've been treated to five wonderful stories of the DO NOT DISTURB series, created by a team of talented authors, beginning with Jo Leigh's *Hush* and ending with Jill Shalvis's *Room Service*. You've met the trendy staff, visited the phenomenal suites and drooled over the delectable offerings of Amuse Bouche.

Now it's my turn to introduce you to Madison Tate and Jack Logan. Neither of whom believes in psychics. Boy, are they in for a surprise.

Come on. Visit us at Hushhotel.com and join the party.

Love,

Debbi Rawlins

HOT SPOT

BY
DEBBI RAWLINS

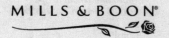

MILLS & BOON®

Mom and Dad, I love and miss you.
Aloha until we meet again.

First published in Great Britain 2007
by Harlequin Mills & Boon Limited, Eton House,
18-24 Paradise Road,
Richmond, Surrey TW9 1SR

© Debbi Quattrone 2005

ISBN: 978 0 263 85563 0

14-0307

Printed and bound in Spain
by Litografia Rosés S.A., Barcelona

Prologue

MADISON TATE LEANED a hip against the wall and peered into the crowded living room of the chic SoHo brownstone, mentally berating herself for getting talked into another party full of meaningless chitchat and men who were prettier than she was.

Of course, it was Friday night and what else would she and Karrie be doing? Except for stuffing their faces with popcorn at one of the cheap theaters or trying to get two-fer tickets for something Off Broadway. And then only if Madison had had a photo gig so she could afford a night out. At least the party circuit was free with plenty of food and enough variety of flavored martinis to give her a headache for a week.

Actually, she should be grateful that the invites kept coming. Neither she nor Karrie were the Dolce & Gabbana type, and they sure as heck didn't make the kind of bucks that most of the other guests did, but about two years ago, they'd met Nancy Kragen, a high-powered book editor, and they'd been on the B+ list ever since.

Madison didn't know what it was about tonight that made her edgy. Probably the news she'd gotten earlier, but no, that didn't make sense. For heaven's sake, the hors d'oeuvres were exceptionally good, the high-end stuff mixed with retro junk food like pigs-in-a-blanket, which were to die for. And Karrie had kept her laughing with tales of petty office bureaucracy and juicy gossip for the past half hour, which as a freelance photographer Madison missed out on, but the restless feeling wouldn't quit.

She looked over at Karrie, thoughtfully sipping a martini, her gaze riveted to the door to Sonya's bedroom, and said, "You don't believe in that nonsense, do you?"

"Of course not."

The door opened and Karrie ducked to get a look at the infamous Madam Zora. Last month it had been a candle party, the month before that, a roll-your-own-sushi night. Tonight Sonya had hired a psychic, of all things. A psychic with no imagination. Madam Zora. Please.

Karrie got that mischievous look in her eyes that meant trouble. "Are you going to sign up for a reading?"

Madison made a face. "I'm not wasting my time."

"As if you have anything better to do." Karrie glanced around the room, her expression dismal. What few men there were had already paired up with women wearing skirts with hemlines up to Canada. "Come on. We're here. I can't bear to go home yet. You know what night this is, right?"

"Ah, yes. The ever-popular Mr. Warzowski's night for screaming at his wife as he goes through two cases of Rolling Rock beer."

"You've gotta love three-floor walkups with paper-thin walls."

"That are more expensive than most five-bedroom houses in any other state."

"But at least the heat doesn't work in the winter and there's none of that noisy air-conditioning in the summer."

Madison nodded and had another big sip of martini. "Well, doll, it's tough for us young, gorgeous career gals."

Karrie's brows rose. "Gorgeous?"

"Hey," Madison said, "if we can't play pretend, I really am leaving." Karrie *was* gorgeous, even though she'd deny it. All that fabulous auburn hair with natural golden highlights, while Madison's dirty-blond hair was so nondescript it was pathetic.

"Which is exactly why we're going to see Madam Zora."

"Oh, no."

"Oh, yes. You and I. Together."

Madison shook her head. "I don't know what Sonya was thinking."

"Probably trying to take our minds off the fact that we have a better chance of winning the lottery than we do of getting lucky tonight." Karrie sipped her peach martini, her gaze drawn to a tall woman with dark waist-length hair and red lipstick who'd emerged from the room.

Madison watched, too, as the woman's dramatically made-up eyes widened when Nancy asked her what happened with the psychic.

"She's amazing. Totally awesome." The woman, whom Madison didn't recognize as a regular, shook her head, her expression a haze of disbelief. "She knew everything about me. Even that I'm engaged."

Madison poked Karrie in the ribs, then nodded at the rock on the woman's finger. "Amazing."

Karrie pressed her lips together but couldn't quite hide her smile. "Come on, you chicken. What can it hurt?"

"Don't make me do this. I hate this kind of stuff. You know I break out in hives when I'm exposed to too much schlock in one evening."

Karrie laughed. "Madison, don't be such a wet blanket. Who knows, maybe she's going to see a tall, handsome stranger in your future."

"Yeah, right."

"Okay, so she won't. But do it, anyway. Please?"

"Fine."

"Okay, then."

Madison caught a passing waiter and exchanged her empty glass for another martini.

"You're really not nervous about this?"

"Of course not. It's all nonsense."

Karrie grinned. "Good. Because I put our names down an hour ago. We're next."

Madison glared at her, but quickly switched her attention to the opening door and Camilla, who'd hosted the candle party last month, her face flushed, the sparkle in her eyes an odd mixture of fear and excitement. Scary. The woman was pretty savvy and not the type to fall for this twaddle.

Karrie made an odd, throaty noise and Madison glanced over at her. She looked as if she might be having second thoughts. Good. Madison didn't want to be a wienie about this, but she didn't want to hear some horrible prediction that her life was about to take a dive or, worse, her career.

Even if it was all nonsense.

"Hey, Madison, Karrie." Sonya waved them toward her bedroom. "Madam Zora is waiting for you."

HER FRIEND LED THE WAY into the dimly lit room, and Madison followed, her pulse accelerating. Silly, since she didn't believe in this stuff. Not even a smidgen. But she had to admit, Sonya had done a good job of setting the mood. She'd put up curtains to hide her bed, and made the area for the reading intimate and exotic, the only light coming from the soft glow of a pair of candles.

"Do not be nervous, now. Come sit." Madam Zora motioned them to the two chairs opposite her, her smile displaying the flash of a gold tooth. She had to be in her forties, or maybe even fifties. Her unlined skin hid her age well, but she had old eyes.

Kind eyes that, amazingly, seemed to put them both at ease.

They were dark, her hair short and as black as the caftan she wore over her large, languid form as she lounged on a burgundy velvet love seat. If not for the giant gold hoops gleaming from her ears, she nearly blended into the black-draped walls.

Karrie sat first, and then gave Madison the eye as if she thought Madison might bolt. Which wasn't a bad idea. Instead she didn't even try to hide her reluctance as she sank into the other chair.

Madam Zora laughed softly. "Tell me why you've come to see Madam Zora," the woman said, looking directly at Karrie.

She shrugged and said bluntly, "This isn't something I'd normally do. I don't really believe in this stuff, but I figured that since you're here and I'm not paying for it…"

Madam Zora laughed again. "You needn't fear me. You have a very bright future...."

Karrie leaned forward with interest.

Madison sighed to herself and listened with half an ear while Karrie continued to get her reading. Mostly general stuff that could apply to anyone. Except halfway through, Madam Z. said some things that caught Madison's full attention. Things the hokey psychic shouldn't have known about Karrie or her brother.

Madison's gaze went to Karrie, and suddenly it wasn't so amusing. She could see from her friend's expression that she was buying every prognostication as gospel. Which wasn't like Karrie at all. This had to be a trick, that's all. Or someone had tipped Madam Zora off about Karrie's brother. It was stupid to even consider...

The second they were finished, Madison stood. Karrie didn't budge, and Madison touched her shoulder. "Come on, kiddo."

Karrie hesitated, but then finally stood, and gave Madam Z. the perfunctory thanks. Madison headed straight for the door.

"You needn't be afraid."

The psychic's voice stopped her in her tracks. She turned back to face the woman, who, come on, could have come up with something more original than the damn gypsy garb. "I'm not. I realize this is only entertainment." At least she didn't call it schlock but she almost reconsidered at the hint of condescension in the older woman's smile. "You have a waiting list. I'll give someone else a turn."

"Ah, but don't you want to hear about the career opportunity on your horizon?"

That got Madison's attention.

"Let's hear her out." Karrie started to go back to her seat.

Madison tugged on her sleeve. "Nah, go ahead. I'll be right behind you."

Karrie gave her a funny look and left. Madison hesitated. Career opportunity was a broad statement. Still, she'd gotten some startling news today…

Ah, hell.

Even as she headed back to take the hot seat, she knew she was being an idiot. "Go on."

Madam Zora nodded. "You have a bright future. Your work will soon become well-known."

Damn it, but Madison suddenly wanted to believe. "Do you know what kind of work I do?"

The woman briefly closed her eyes. "You tell stories," she said, and Madison smirked. So much for that. "With pictures," Madam Zora added.

Madison gaped. How in the hell… Sonya could have told her. Probably gave Zora a heads-up on all the guests. Made for better entertainment.

The psychic smiled, almost as if she knew what Madison was thinking. Ridiculous.

"There is adventure awaiting you. Places and things you have never seen, experiences far out of your imagination."

"I see."

"You will share this with a man."

"Ah."

The psychic briefly closed her eyes. The effect was lost on Madison. "He is someone who works with you."

Madison sighed. She freelanced, for heaven's sake.

Why had she bothered wasting her time? Even if she didn't have anything better to do.

"But you don't know him." Madam Z. frowned. "Yet."

"Right."

One of the woman's brows went up. "It's up to you whether you believe or not."

"That's right."

"So choose to believe this." Madam Zora leaned slightly forward. "There are things you hold dear that you must let go. Nothing will bring you the satisfaction you seek until you open your mind. A broken heart need not be."

Madison sighed. "Thank you," she said, rising from her seat, ready to get back to her martini. She knew now that the so-called psychic was just blowing smoke. She'd known about Madison's profession because she'd done her homework, not because she had supernatural gifts. "You're good," she said, meaning it. It must have taken her quite some time to research all the guests.

Madam Zora laughed. "Yes, and so are you," she said. "But that skill won't be enough to get you what you want." She paused until Madison got to the door. "There's more."

Madison smiled, then got the hell out of the room.

Karrie waited impatiently outside. "Hey, hey. What was that about 'I'll be right behind you'?"

"Okay, I was an idiot. I stayed an extra minute. It was garbage, Karrie."

"Garbage? Did you hear what she said about my brother?"

"She did her homework, I'll give you that, but as for the rest? She got one thing right about me. That's it."

"That you're a photographer?"

Madison shook her head. "Nope. That I got a new job."

"A job? Like going in from nine-to-five?"

She shook her head. "Okay, it's an assignment, so she didn't get that right, either."

Karrie squinted. "Not for—"

Madison nodded. "For *Today's Man.*"

"No way. Which issue?"

She grinned at her best bud.

Karrie stepped back. "The sexiest-man layout?"

"Yep."

"Oh, my God. That's terrific! When were you going to tell me?"

"I got the call this afternoon. I still can't believe it myself."

Karrie raised her glass. "Congratulations. Damn."

"Save the kudos until I get the man-of-the-year cover."

Karrie sighed. "Would you chill out long enough to enjoy the moment? This is major. World class. How many photographers vie for that shoot each month? And you got it."

"Yeah, but—"

"Nope." She held up a hand. "I'm not listening to any 'yeah buts.' You're too hard on yourself. You're a damn good photographer, and you deserve the assignment. Period. Which state are you covering?"

"New York. I'm shooting right here in Manhattan."

"Cool. Who's the guy?"

"That's up to me."

"I know you have someone in mind."

"A couple of guys, actually, but I have over a month before I have to submit a name."

"Are you going to give me a hint?" Karrie waited during the span of a leisurely sip. "I'll give you one. The question was rhetorical."

Madison laughed. Yeah, she had one guy in particular in mind. But he wasn't going to be easy. Others had tried to snag him to no avail. "I'm superstitious. I don't want to jinx it."

"Oh, brother." Karrie sighed. "Okay, I'm sure you'll find someone positively delicious."

"Delicious?" Madison sipped her drink again, wishing it was later so they could head home. "I just pray that he's photogenic, and not an insufferable prick."

"Who knows," Kerrie said, her brows arching. "Maybe you won't find his prick insufferable at all."

1

Three Months Later...

"EXCUSE ME, JACK, but there's a Madison Tate on line two for you." Lana stood expectantly at his office door, pushing the mass of shiny black hair away from her face. "She says you're expecting her call."

Jack Logan hesitated. He should talk to her and get it over with. The sooner he got the eager Ms. Tate off his back the better. "Take a message, will you, Lana?"

"Sure." She smiled, first at him and then at Larry before turning to leave, her short skirt showing off a pair of dynamite legs.

Shaking his graying head, Larry exhaled sharply as he tapped the edge of Jack's desk. "I don't think my heart could take having a secretary who looked like that."

Jack smiled at his longtime agent. "She has a husband and twin toddlers she adores."

"With those eyes and that smile she should be working in front of the camera. Maybe I ought to try and sign her up—"

"She's not interested. She's just a nice kid from Nebraska who can't wait to get home to her kids every day." Jack loosened his tie and motioned with his chin to the briefcase on Larry's lap. "You have papers for me to review?"

Larry stared back, his weathered face creasing into a frown. Years of golf without sun protection had added ten years to him. He suddenly looked grim. "You're not going to like the new contract."

"That's a given. Let me see it."

"Not to say it's not a good deal. It's entirely favorable to you. Any other morning-show host would give his right arm for the concessions they're willing to make. I heard that Matt Lauer couldn't even—"

"Larry, just give me the contract."

The older man sighed and took the leather folder out of his briefcase. "Don't be rash. Think about how much you have to lose."

"Jack?"

They both looked toward Lana standing in the doorway. She made an apologetic face.

"I'm sorry to interrupt you again," she said with a helpless wave of her hand, "but this Madison Tate says she's already left two messages and that it's important."

Jack sighed. *Right.* An important beefcake magazine spread. Talk about an oxymoron. Pictures of insurgents' victims in the Middle East, earthquake victims in India—now, that defined the word *important*.

"You haven't returned her calls?" Larry gave him a stern look. "If you want to leave room for negotiation, don't piss off the network."

Jack's jaw clenched. Of course he knew Larry was right. Didn't mean he had to like the idea. "I'll take it, Lana. Thanks."

She glanced at Larry, nodded and then left.

"Consider this a trade-off," Larry said, as Jack reached for the phone. "The network wants this exposure."

"I don't need the sales pitch. I already agreed." Jack started to use his speakerphone and quickly changed his mind. He wanted some illusion of control over this ridiculous publicity stunt his producer and Larry had arranged. He brought the receiver to his ear and depressed the blinking red button. "Jack Logan."

At his brusque tone, Larry shook his head in disgust.

"Madison Tate here," the woman responded equally businesslike. "We haven't talked before, Mr. Logan, so I'll take this opportunity to thank you for agreeing to this photo shoot. Now, let's talk about a time and place."

Jack half smiled. She knew how to get to the point. "I assume you already have a place in mind."

"At Hush. It's that hot new boutique hotel located in midtown owned by Piper Devon. I'm sure you've heard of it."

His smile faded. "Yes, I have."

"You sound annoyed."

"Why there?"

"It's not only the hippest place in Manhattan right now, but the decor is gorgeous."

He briefly closed his eyes. Yeah, he knew the place. He knew Piper, too. Nice lady. But from the day it opened, the hotel had attracted its share of scandal, a field day for the press, who'd labeled it the sex hotel.

"Mr. Logan?"

"Yeah, I'm here." He glanced at Larry, who listened with far too much interest. "Let's talk about that further. Maybe we could meet for a drink."

"Okay," she said slowly, "but we'll have to start

shooting soon. I'm sure you can appreciate that I have a deadline."

"Of course." He opened the jar of jellybeans he kept on his desk. "I'll check my schedule and—"

"How about this evening?"

He paused, his hand halfway into the jar. For a moment he thought about blowing her off. Telling her he'd call back tomorrow, but his grudging appreciation of her no-nonsense approach stopped him. "What time?"

"Your call."

"Six."

"Perfect."

"Where?"

"Hush. At the bar. I look forward to it, Mr. Logan." She hung up before he could say a word.

He shook his head as he replaced the phone.

"What?" Larry leaned forward, his brows drawn together. Made Jack wonder if the man was born with a frown. Even when the guy smiled he still looked as if he were troubled about something.

He was a good agent, though, and always frank. Didn't mouth what Jack wanted to hear. Just told it like it was. No behind-the-back deals. No back stabbing. He'd been with Jack from the beginning and was loyal to a fault.

Many of Jack's peers had advised him to change agents. Claimed Larry was a dinosaur. Even a couple of Jack's producers thought he should have a new hip young agent. But he had little use for the brash, flashy upstarts who thought schmoozing was more important than good reporting. Besides, loyalty went both ways.

"You've met her, right? After you and Ernie were approached by *Today's Man?*"

"Madison Tate's not with *Today's Man.* She's a free-lancer. And yeah, I met her."

"A freelancer? You've got to be kidding." He stared at Larry, wanting to seriously strangle the guy. The major magazine had astronomical circulation numbers that couldn't be ignored. He could see why the network had twisted his arm to do the layout, but… "You sold me out to a damn freelancer?"

"Number one, I did not sell you out. This is a good career move. Number two, the agreement is for *Today's Man*'s sexiest man article only." Larry shrugged. "Besides, hard to say no to a woman like that."

Jack leaned back, testing the limit of his leather chair, and scrubbed at his jaw. Sighing, he came back to face Larry, shaking his head. "I never thought I'd see the day a pretty face could influence your business decisions."

Larry scoffed. "You never will. This Tate is all right in the looks department, tall, thin, short dirty-blond hair, nothing special, but she's got grit, one of those real go-getters, doesn't understand the word *no.* But she doesn't cross the line, either. Reminds me of you when you were younger."

When he was younger… Jack stiffened. Larry had struck a raw nerve. Nothing to do with age. Jack was only thirty-six. But his recent complacency was starting to bother him. He'd let celebrity and money take center stage. He'd been ambitious once, single-mindedly chasing after the story of the century. Nothing could have stopped him in those days. Not even a multi-million-dollar contract.

"So where does she want the shoot to take place?" Larry got to his feet and predictably pinched the crease down the front of his slacks. "She hadn't chosen a location when Ernie and I spoke to her. We left it open but that you'd have final say."

"Hush."

Larry's eyes gleamed. "Brilliant choice. See? The woman's got savvy."

"Yeah, just what my image needs." Bad enough he was considered the pretty boy of the network, of the morning infotainment show no less, a bona fide heart-throb according to the media. He hated it.

With a hint of a smile on his face, Larry laid the leather folders on Jack's desk. "Talk to her and let me know what happens."

"I can tell you right now what'll happen."

Larry sighed. "Read the contract later. You don't need to meet Tate with an attitude."

Jack watched the older man leave. He walked with a slight stoop Jack hadn't noticed before. The guy had never mentioned his age but he had to be in his mid-sixties, and he still worked just as hard as he had when he took Jack on as a client fourteen years ago. He clearly loved his job and gave it a hundred and fifty percent.

Jack's gaze went to the leather folder. Would he be able to say the same in thirty years?

AS SOON AS MADISON HUNG UP the phone, she let out a yowl. She stomped her feet a few times, going in a circle, doing the happy dance and then sank into the swivel chair she'd nearly sent flying across the small office.

Nearby, Talia looked up from the article she'd been editing and peered over her thick, black-rimmed glasses.

"You arranged a meet," she said in her usual monotone voice. "Just a guess."

Out of breath, Madison nodded. Talia was good people, in spite of her odd sense of humor and even odder taste in clothes, and she did let Madison use her office sometimes, but, man, Madison wished Karrie were here.

Madison missed her like crazy on a normal basis but at a time like this it was really hard to have her best friend living all the way across the country. Not that she wasn't happy that Karrie had found Rob, but jeez… It had been months since Karrie had moved west to be with her guy.

She glanced at her watch. Two-fifteen, which made it eleven-fifteen Las Vegas time. She wouldn't call yet. She'd wait until after she met with him. *The* Jack Logan. She still couldn't quite wrap her brain around the magnitude of snaring someone like the heart-stopping Logan.

Talia snorted. "If I hadn't seen it with my own eyes, I wouldn't have believed it."

"What?"

"You acting like a star-struck teenager."

Madison laughed. "He's only the sexiest man in the western hemisphere."

Talia shook her head. "I still don't believe it."

"The only thing Jack Logan means to me is the cover of your magazine." Madison locked her hands behind her head, leaned back and stretched her legs out. Wait until the other photographers found out whom she'd snagged. They'd drool like babies. Cry their eyes out. Or want to scratch hers out. An ugly thought struck her, and she looked at Talia. "Heard anything about who the other men are?"

"Nope. Nothing. Oh, wait, I did hear that Sheila Higgins might have Brad Pitt on the hook."

Madison shot upright. "No way."

Talia just shrugged.

"Big deal. He's been on so many covers. Old news. I'm not worried."

Talia smiled. "Yeah, I can tell by the way you nearly hit the ceiling. Relax, kid. I was kidding. I haven't heard a word."

"Go ahead, make fun." Madison stood and tucked the loosened white T-shirt into her jeans. "Some day you'll say 'I knew her when.'"

Talia put down her pencil and cocked her head to the side. "Say you get the cover. Then what?"

Madison stared in disbelief. "No more begging for assignments, or sitting at the bottom of slush piles. I get to write my own ticket. I mean, getting to shoot the cover is a pretty damn big deal."

"Oh, yeah. Definitely a major career coup." Talia's dark eyes bore into hers. "My question is, what does writing your own ticket mean?"

Madison looked blankly at her and then shrugged. "More freedom."

"To do what?"

"Pay my bills, for one." Madison snorted. "Get to choose my own assignments. Why?"

"No reason." Talia gave her a small mysterious smile, her dark red lips barely curving.

"You know something I don't?"

Talia just shook her head. "Just curious."

Madison grabbed her navy blue blazer off the back of the chair, a sudden unease quelling her excitement.

"I don't want to take celebrity photos for the rest of my life."

"You're very talented, Madison, you certainly don't have to." Talia paused, and then added, "If that's not what you want."

"For now it works for me. It's something I know I can do well." She shrugged into her blazer. "Maybe later I'll branch out. After I put a few bucks away. Just not yet."

"No need to get defensive."

"I'm not." Madison knew that was a lie. Even her posture had turned defensive. Silly, really. No reason for it. Everything she said was true. She was happy. This was the break she'd been waiting for. "Well, I'd better go get ready. We're meeting in two hours."

"Hmm. You have time for a color and blow dry." Talia frowned at Madison's short, uneven nails. "No, get a manicure instead."

"You're hysterical." She picked up her portfolio that contained a recent head shot of Logan and a brief bio she'd found on the Internet.

She figured she ought to know a little something about him other than he had a face and body that gave even her elderly grandmother heart palpitations.

"You coming by tomorrow?" Talia took off her glasses and rubbed her eyes.

"Probably, but it kind of depends on tonight."

Talia grinned. "I'm jealous."

Yeah, right. As if. Madison sighed. "You're hopeless."

"You know what would be a real kick?"

"Do I want to hear this?"

"Remember that psychic you went to?"

"Don't even go there." Madison headed for the door.

"Anyway, I didn't go to see her. She was at a party. It was stupid."

"I'm just saying…" Talia's eyes widened. "Hey, didn't your friend Karrie's prediction come true?"

Madison's hand froze on the doorknob. She'd been so wrapped up in getting this assignment she'd forgotten. Not that Karrie's or her prediction meant anything. Coincidence of course.

Even so…

Jack Logan? No way.

JACK ARRIVED AT EROTIQUE ten minutes early, but she was already there. He knew it was Madison Tate sitting at a small table near the black circular bar. Not just because she was the only woman sitting alone. The voice on the phone matched this woman perfectly. The way she was dressed, the way she sat with her back straight and her head held high. No-nonsense.

While the other women in the bar were decked out in the latest fall offerings from Prada or Bebe, she dressed simply in jeans and a white T-shirt, generic, not designer. Her dark-blond hair wasn't particularly stylish, either. Kind of short and unruly, and before he crossed the room, her long slender fingers pushed the stubborn locks away from her face twice.

The moment she saw him she stood and smiled. A nice friendly smile. Not the kind he usually got from women.

"You're early," she said and offered her hand.

He accepted the firm handshake. "You're earlier."

"Bad habit of mine." She reclaimed her seat, and he took off his overcoat and sat across from her, laying the expensive coat across his lap.

"My mother used to say that being prompt or early shows respect. Being late indicates you think your time is more valuable than the other person's." He didn't have the faintest idea why he'd elaborated like that. But when her mouth stretched into a beautiful smile he was glad he had.

"Your mama sounds like a wise woman."

"Yes, she was."

"Oh." Her smile faded. "I'm sorry. I lost mine, too. Last year. It was really hard. Still is."

"Yeah. My mom passed away while I was in college. Seems like yesterday."

An awkward silence settled for a few moments, and then they both spoke at once.

Madison grinned. "Go ahead."

Two women sitting at a table behind Madison stared blatantly at him. He was used to the intrusion. Came with the territory. But this pair particularly annoyed him, especially the redhead, who gave him one of those silly four-fingered waves. "I'm sorry. What were you saying?"

A slight frown puckered Madison's brows. "Here comes the waitress. Know what you want?"

What he wanted and what his personal trainer allowed were two different things. Ah, what the hell. "Scotch," he told the young woman in the pink vest. "Neat."

"Right away." She looked barely twelve, although she obviously had to be over twenty-one. "Would you like another club soda?" she asked Madison.

"I'm good." She waited until the waitress moved away, and then said, "You gotta admit, this place is amazing."

Jack glanced at the unique, black-lacquered circular bar, awash in a rosy glow from the pink overhead lights. The bar chairs with the inverted triangular backs were chic and surprisingly comfortable from what he remembered of the grand opening. The entire hotel was a class act. That didn't mean he wanted to be associated with the place. "No argument there."

Her eyebrows rose. "But?"

He shrugged a shoulder. "What do you want me to say?"

"That you'll do the photo shoot here."

He smiled. "Why not Central Park?"

"Because it's November and you're likely to freeze you're a—behind off."

"It's not that cold yet."

"You won't say that after we've been outside for six hours."

"Six hours?"

"If we're lucky."

"Well, let's make sure we're real lucky."

Her expression tightened, and she lifted her drink to her lips.

After a brief silence, he said, "I understand this isn't just about me. It's about the city. Isn't that the first thing people think of when you mention Manhattan?"

She gave him a funny look. "They probably think of the Statue of Liberty." Then quickly added, "And no, we're not doing it there."

"I guess that leaves out two places."

Annoyance flashed in her light-brown eyes. "I don't understand why it matters. It's not like I'm asking you to run naked through Times Square."

The waitress had reappeared and she'd obviously heard given the way her eyes widened slightly. "Excuse me." She smiled at Jack. "The ladies at the next table would like to buy you a drink, Mr. Logan."

He shook his head, his gaze staying on Madison. "Tell them thanks anyway, but it doesn't look as if I'll be staying long."

Meeting his eyes, Madison didn't seem the least bit intimidated. Angry, maybe. Frustrated, definitely.

Unaware of the undercurrent, the waitress said, "I'm sorry I didn't recognize you earlier, Mr. Logan. Between this job and school I don't have much time to watch the news. Not that kind, anyway."

He switched his gaze in time to see her oblivious smile before she walked away. *Not that kind.* Her words stayed behind, taunting him, reminding him of how many people didn't consider him a serious newsman. To them he was just a pretty face, delivering national news, joking with his coanchor and providing entertainment while the television audience sipped their morning coffee.

"I have an idea," Madison said, her nervousness betrayed by the way her fingers continuously circled the glass.

"I'm listening."

"After our drink, why don't we go for a walk around the hotel and—"

"I've already seen it."

"All of it?"

"At the opening."

"Ah." She sighed, sinking back. "Of course." And then she straightened and leaned toward him with renewed determination on her face. "So? Is the place stunning or what?"

"Was that rhetorical?"

"Absolutely."

He had to smile. She had a fascinatingly expressive face. A moment before she spoke he could tell what she was thinking. She wouldn't make it a day in his business where everyone maintained a poker face. They had to. Never let them see you sweat. He'd learned the lesson early on.

For a second he regretted that they couldn't come to terms. He wouldn't mind working with her. But this obviously was a bad idea. The whole shoot celebrated an image he was trying to get away from. He shook his head. "This isn't going to work. I'm sorry I wasted your time."

2

MADISON EYED HIM for a moment, trying to decide her best approach. Getting angry would obviously get her nowhere, no matter how much she wanted to tell him to get off his high horse. The waitress arrived with his drink, which gave Madison another few moments to consider pointing out that his agent and producer had both, on his behalf, agreed to this magazine spread.

Nah, too antagonistic. She didn't need him getting defensive. She wanted his complete cooperation. Besides, it was apparent his agent had couched the truth. The spread had nothing to do with Manhattan and everything to do with the sex appeal of the man sitting across from her. And, oh, baby, was she sitting on a gold mine. She was going to kick ass. Make the other photographers seethe with envy.

But she had to be careful. His agent had confided that Jack Logan valued his privacy. That his initial response had been an unequivocal no. What had changed his mind, she had no idea. All she knew was that she couldn't have him backing out now.

She watched him flash that million-dollar smile at the waitress, and had to swallow. He truly was beautiful. With those keen hazel eyes that danced with just enough amusement and the kind of daring that could make a girl leap before she looked.

Madison considered herself fairly immune to pretty faces, but even she carefully avoided gazing too long for fear of getting off track, forgetting her goal. He was a meal ticket for her. Nothing more. Anyway, guys like him didn't go for women like her, which made it easier to stay focused. Most of the time.

He pushed his fingers through his light-brown hair, and for a second she was tempted to ask the burning question. The one that always came up in the gossip columns. The one he always rebuffed. Was there someone special who got to run their fingers through those golden highlights?

As soon as the waitress left, Madison said, "Okay, let's discuss Central Park. Midday lighting would be best." She nibbled thoughtfully on her lower lip. Like hell they'd shoot there. Or anywhere outside. She was getting at least two shots with his shirt off, or her name wasn't Madison Marie Tate. "Of course, a lot of people eat lunch there. Any later and people will be commuting or jogging. That's okay. We can shoot around them."

He paused to stare at her over his glass, and then downed the scotch.

Damn, she hoped he didn't order another one too quickly. The drinks were coming out of her pocket, and at fourteen dollars a pop… God, if her credit card was maxed out she'd kick herself.

"The park's a big place. Surely we can find some privacy."

"Maybe. But we can't shoot in only one spot, we need a variety of backdrops, and we're bound to attract some attention." She smiled. "Of course, you're used to being in the public eye. That shouldn't bother you."

His face tightened. Damn. Even frowning he looked good. "Where else did you have in mind?"

"Well, your studio might be interesting. A shot of you in your office, one on the set."

He thoughtfully pursed his lips, looking entirely too interested in the idea.

"There won't always be staff around, right?" she added quickly. "I will have to pose you at times, and well, I wouldn't want you to be uncomfortable with an audience."

"Pose me?"

"Of course."

He thought for a moment. "No, not the studio."

"Okay…" She paused for effect, and shifted her legs. Their knees touched under the table, and the awareness that sparked nearly threw her off track. "Sorry."

"My fault." He winced as he moved his legs to the side. "You okay?"

"What? Yeah, old war wound."

"Oh. You were in the service?"

One side of his mouth lifted. "Close. I was a field reporter back in the day."

"Right." She remembered reading his bio. "The Gulf War. Your first big assignment out of college." The one that had launched his career, she almost said, but something in his grim expression warned her to drop the subject.

"You had another idea for a location?" he prompted.

She smiled sweetly. "How about your apartment?"

"I have a house."

"Better yet. Where?"

"That's out."

"Why? We'd have privacy. People would love getting a peek into your private domain."

He grunted. "Not going to happen."

She'd actually started warming to the idea, and threw up her hands. "Then what's your suggestion?"

He studied her for a long uncomfortable moment. Made her want to check her teeth. Take a swipe at her cheek in case something god-awful clung to her skin. Finally he said, "You're manipulating me."

She opened her mouth to deny it. "Is it working?"

He smiled, briefly, and then shook his head. "What about another hotel? The Plaza? The Waldorf Astoria?"

"They're stuffy. They don't suit your image."

"And Hush does?"

"Absolutely."

He didn't look happy.

"Look." She leaned forward. "I know you don't like the sex symbol image. Your agent told me. But that's part of what's earning you the big bucks."

Frowning, he broke eye contact and stared down at his empty glass.

"Hey, it's not like I'm shooting a *Playgirl* layout," Madison said, her confidence beginning to slip. If he backed out now, she'd be so screwed. "My name is gonna be attached to this. I'm motivated to keep the photos tasteful."

He looked up and studied her for a long, uncomfortable moment. "You won't make a big production out of the hotel."

"Nope. You're the star attraction. *Today's Man* is a

woman's magazine, and every female head turned when you walked in."

"I didn't notice," he muttered.

"You're used to it." She shrugged, amazed that even the sudden scowl didn't detract from his good looks. "That's probably part of your appeal."

"Are you always this frank?"

Madison nodded. "It saves a lot of time."

His lips curved suddenly, surprising her, and unleashing a mass of butterflies in her stomach. The smile reached his eyes and they actually seemed to change color right before her, going from cool green to warm amber. "Okay, Hush it is."

"Yeah?" She smiled back, words deserting her. Unusual for her. But there was something about this man…

"But…" He held up a finger as if admonishing a naughty child. Even his hands were noteworthy. Tan, with lean fingers and evenly clipped nails. No prissy manicure.

"I'm listening." Barely. Her stomach was just beginning to calm down.

"I still have veto power."

"Of course." Her gaze went again to his hands, to that perfect golden color, so perfect it had to be artificial.

He squinted with suspicion. "What?"

"Are you tanned all over?"

His head reared back slightly.

"That's strictly a professional question," Madison said, and pressed her lips together to keep from laughing at his appalled expression.

She didn't get her answer. The waitress reappeared to see if they wanted another round, and to ask for his autograph on behalf of a woman seated behind Madison. Jack turned down another scotch, smiled graciously and took the pen and napkin from the waitress.

Madison studied his bent head as he signed his name. The highlights were natural, she decided, probably from the sun. His hair was already getting darker consistent with the fall weather that restricted outdoor activity. Just like her, in fact. She was always blonder in the summer. Except the sun wasn't as creative or kind to her.

He looked up and met her eyes.

She smiled. "I'd hate this."

"What?" He handed the napkin and pen back to the waitress who promptly disappeared.

"Being recognized, the intrusions... But I guess it comes with the territory."

"So they tell me," he said flatly, and then smiled briefly at someone over Madison's shoulder. Then, barely moving his lips, he said, "Can we please get out of here?"

"Sure." Madison grabbed her blazer and the camera bag she used as a purse. "Just let me get the check."

He pulled some bills out of his pocket secured by a brushed-gold money clip. "Did you have more than the one club soda?"

"No, but I want to—"

He laid down three twenties. "That should take care of it."

"No, this is on me. Besides, that's way too much."

He laughed humorlessly and stood. "The price of celebrity. Let's go. Now."

She realized what he'd meant as soon as she stood. The redhead, wearing a short white spandex dress with more cleavage than good taste, approached the table. Jack smiled at her, tossed his coat over his shoulder and then took Madison by the elbow to hurry her along.

"Mr. Logan, I wanted to thank you personally for the autograph." The woman smiled, flashing a set of super-white teeth. "I truly hated to bother you."

"No bother." He stopped but his grip on Madison's elbow tightened. "Sorry, but we're in a hurry."

"Of course." The woman gave Madison an odd look, which took her a full twenty seconds to interpret as envy while Jack rushed her out of the intimate bar.

By the time they got to the lobby, she'd nearly hemorrhaged from trying not to laugh. Imagine anyone thinking she was *with* Jack Logan. What a hoot! Wait till she told Karrie and Talia.

"Are you really in a hurry, or was that a smoke screen?" she asked, turning to face him. He was tall but so was she, and standing so close, his incredible face only inches away, well, it literally took her breath away. She inhaled deeply, hopefully not conspicuously. "I'd like to show you some of the places I think would make great shots."

His lips curved slightly and then he glanced at his watch. "My driver is picking me up in half an hour."

"Great. We'll make it a quickie." To her horror, heat crept into her cheeks. Which was totally insane. She never blushed. "Oh, there's Kit. She's in charge of the hotel PR. Let me catch her and get a key."

Madison took off in the woman's direction. This was bad. Really bad. Madison moistened her dry lips. Swallowed hard. No, it was good. If she reacted this way to him, millions of women out there would be drooling over his pictures. Over the cover. And let's face it, if she couldn't snag that cover with him as her subject, she might as well hang up her camera.

Her heart started to race, but this time it wasn't because of a pair of incredible hazel eyes and a killer grin. She could see her star rising.

JACK GOT OUT HIS CELL PHONE and called Dutch and told him to give him another hour before he picked him up. The network provided a car and driver. It was in Jack's contract. One of many great perks that came with the job, he reminded himself. This photo-shoot nonsense was a trade-off. The sooner he got it over with, the better.

It could be worse. At least Madison Tate was a pleasant surprise. She was attractive enough, but it wasn't that. As Larry had warned, there was something compelling about her, some quality that made you want to go along for the ride. Maybe it was her refreshing frankness, or that she wasn't coy or flirtatious. He admired that she had a goal and kept her eyes on the ball. Too bad he was her short-term goal.

He saw her come from the direction of the front desk, and she smiled and held up a key, earning them a second look from a couple waiting for the elevator. He nearly choked wondering if she even knew what that looked like.

"I want to show you the rooftop garden for starters," she said, briskly walking past him, obviously expecting him to follow. "And the pool and spa, and two of the suites that I think would be great possibilities. I'll need to take quite a few shots, of course, and then narrow them down to five. So I'd like to widen our scope and—"

She stopped abruptly and looked over at him. "I know you're in a hurry so I'm trying to make this quick."

"Fine."

"Okay." She took the lead again, and he noticed that she had a slight sway to her hips that was totally unexpected. "We'll start with one of the penthouse suites and the garden, and then work our way down until it's time for you to go."

"Fine." He wished she'd lose the jacket. Give him a clear view of her behind.

"I'm kind of leaning toward spots where we can use the city as a backdrop. Obviously the rooftop garden is perfect but so are the suites and spa because they have views of Midtown or the skyline along the river."

"Fine." He had no doubt she had great legs. Long and lean, and her jeans were short enough that he could see her slim ankles. Generally a good sign.

She stopped again. "Could we have a little more enthusiasm here?"

"I beg your pardon."

"Attitude is great for photographs but right now we need to get down to business," she said, and then looked as if she wished she hadn't. Drawing in her lower lip, she glanced away. "Sorry."

Jack's sparked temper subsided. Not just because of the apology. Or the sexy way she played with her lip. He'd allowed himself to be distracted and lost the thread of the conversation. "I'm sorry," he said. "My mind wandered."

She smiled, shrugged a shoulder. "Just give me a nudge if I'm making you yawn."

He smiled back and they said nothing until they'd

gotten into the elevator and arrived at the roof. He held the cab door and waited for her to precede him. Before he stepped out, a fusion of fragrances reached him. Apparently, a small thing like winter hadn't interrupted the Hush garden.

A retractable glass roof that hadn't been there during the spring opening now enclosed the area making it a greenhouse. The air was almost too balmy. A plethora of scarlet mums and white carnations gave way to a standing fountain. Near a stone bench grew clusters of lavender orchids.

"Amazing, isn't it?" Madison looked at him, her eyes gleaming, and then she hurried to the edge and peered out over the city lights coming to life. "Wouldn't this make an awesome shot?"

"Quite impressive, I have to admit." Plexiglas domed past the railing giving observers a nearly panoramic view of Midtown and all the way to Central Park.

"They have a full-time gardener."

"I'd imagine they'd have to." He didn't know much about flowers, but this assortment in late November? Someone had to work their butt off. Amazing what money could buy.

"That would be Clarissa, the most interesting woman on the planet. She grows herbs for the restaurant in that corner over there." Madison turned back to him, squinting a little when the light shone directly into her face. "See? This hotel is about so much more than sex."

Her makeup was minimal, her skin, smooth, silky, the kind his coanchor had to slave for and frequently complained about. He'd only listened with half an ear.

Skin wasn't what he normally noticed about a woman. He didn't know why he did now.

She looked away, probably because he'd stared too long.

"It's still about sex," he said finally.

She let out an exasperated sound and looked at him again. "How can you say that? This is about attention to detail. Making the place beautiful. Romantic."

"Which is conducive to sex."

"Romance and sex aren't the same things."

He gave her an appalled look. "They aren't?"

A smile tugged at her lips. "Don't be such a guy."

"I'll ignore that sexist remark."

"Thank you. Want to see the pool?"

"Sure."

"It's this way." When she turned, the camera bag hanging on her shoulder swung hard enough to smack his arm. She covered her mouth and murmured, "I'm *so* sorry."

His hand reflexively went to the assaulted area. "What do you have in that thing?"

She gingerly touched his bicep. "I hope I didn't bruise you."

He laughed. "I think I'll live."

"Of course a little makeup would take care of that," she murmured mostly to herself but her warm breath managed to drift across his cheek.

The sudden urge to touch her face really confused him, and he stepped back, afraid his body's reaction might take an embarrassing turn. Only then did her comment sink in. "Makeup? On my arm?"

She nodded and lowered her hand. "For the photos."

He stared at the spot, closer to his shoulder than his elbow, and then met her eyes. "I'm not taking off my shirt."

"You have to."

"I wouldn't bet your camera on it."

3

MADISON WASN'T ABOUT to argue. He would take off his shirt when the time was right. So far she'd been able to coax even the most reluctant subject to comply with her requests, be it to smile or show a little skin. Nothing too risqué. Just tantalizing. He'd be no different, as long as she didn't blow it by shooting off her big mouth. She knew better than to bring up the issue. But for a moment he'd gotten her so damn flustered she couldn't think straight.

It wasn't just her. There was definitely a *je ne sais quoi* thing happening with him. A mysterious appeal that couldn't be defined by mortal beings. It was just there.

"I only meant that if we take a shot with you in the pool or spa—" She shrugged and smiled when his expression darkened. "Forget I said that. Let's go."

She headed for the pool without glancing back, hoping like hell he followed. She didn't have a lot of time to get her photos in to *Today's Man,* and with his schedule he probably had even less time to pose for them. It wasn't as if they had a contract. If he were to suddenly withdraw...

Her stomach clenched. She couldn't even bring herself to think about that.

"Madison? Slow down."

She swallowed and then turned to face him. "Yes?"

"Let's skip the pool."

"It's just right there." She pointed. "Have you seen the bottom? It's a mosaic of black and pink tiles and the same Plexiglas roof—"

He didn't look happy as he glanced at his watch. "I have only twenty minutes."

"Right. Okay. Let's go look at one of the suites." She knew what he was doing. Warning her not to waste time with the pool because he wouldn't be removing his shirt. Fine. There was always the spa.

The elevator trip down to the eighteenth floor was short and silent. His mood had definitely shifted, and Madison decided it would be wise to give as little information as possible for now. Once they started the shoot, she'd get him relaxed and more amenable to her suggestions.

Using the card key, she opened the double doors to the penthouse suite, three thousand square feet of sheer decadence. One night in this pleasure palace would cost her the equivalent of five months' rent.

The foyer alone was huge, massive, and the floor an incredible Italian marble that made her want to tiptoe across so she wouldn't leave a single mark. On the walls hung Warhol originals that Madison had already drooled over when Janice Foster, the hotel's manager, had graciously given Madison the tour yesterday.

"Not bad, huh?" She grinned at Jack. "They call this the Pop Suite. Two bedrooms, three baths, with butler service." She sighed. "I suppose I could have my arm twisted."

He smiled and strolled over to look at the artwork. "I didn't see this one during the opening."

"I've only seen two other penthouse suites. One being the bridal suite, so I don't think we'll be doing a photo spread there."

"I'm surprised." Amusement tugged at the corners of his mouth. "I figured that would be your first choice."

"You're supposed to be the city's most eligible bachelor. The last thing I want to do is dispel the fantasy."

He turned away, the smile gone. Clearly he hadn't considered that angle, and like a damn fool, she'd pointed it out. He went to the window and stared out at the skyline, and she quietly went to stand beside him.

"Amazing city, huh?" she said, glancing sideways at him. Great profile. Straight nose. Strong jaw. Her heart foolishly skipped a beat.

"That it is."

"Are you from here?"

He looked at her, briefly, probably wondering if she'd read his bio...which she had, but now with his gaze on hers, she couldn't remember detail one as he turned his attention back to the glittering symphony of lights. "Nebraska."

"No kidding."

"No kidding," he repeated. "Know where that is?"

"Midwest."

A hint of a smile lifted his lips. "Close enough."

"Do you miss it?"

He turned back to her again, an odd look on his face. Oh, no. Now what had she said wrong?

"I had to think for a moment," he said. "That's not a typical question."

"And here I thought I was being so cliché."

He really smiled, causing that flutter in her chest again. She silently cleared her throat. "So? Do you?"

"You'd make a hell of an interviewer. You don't give up."

"I've been accused of persistence on occasion."

"Not a bad quality."

"Depends on who you ask." She shrugged and moved away from the window, becoming increasingly aware of his nearness. Of the way his chin was starting to shadow…of the attractive crease in his cheek when he smiled. "If you don't want to talk about your family that's fine."

"They're all still in Omaha and I go back to see them about once a year. My parents and I have a great relationship, so there's no dirt to dig up."

Nothing in the world annoyed her more than to be associated with paparazzi in even the tiniest way. "Frankly, I don't care if you sleep with your sister. I take celebrity photos. The only thing that interests me is capturing your sex appeal on film."

His jaw tightened, and at the moment he looked a lot angrier than he did sexy. He consulted his watch, probably to keep from shooting daggers at her. "I think we've had enough fun for one evening."

Regret restored her common sense. "Don't you want to look at the rest of the suite?"

"Not particularly."

"Then you have no objection to shooting in here?"

He glanced toward the bedroom. From their vantage point, they could glimpse the cherrywood four-poster bed.

"Come see in here," she said, heading for the bedroom door. "It'll just take a minute."

"Why?" he asked even as he approached her. "How many settings do you need? How many shots will you be taking?"

She wasn't about to tell him how many rolls of film she'd been known to take to get just the right shot. Instead she shrugged and continued toward the door. "This room is unreal. We're already here. You should at least see it."

Reluctantly he followed her into the huge bedroom that was bigger than her entire flat. The deep burgundy walls and velvet chaise should have made the room look more traditional, but somehow didn't. It helped that the crystal chandelier was totally modern, a work of art, in fact, and that the room offered every convenience known to man.

And then some.

Her gaze automatically went to the armoire—a virtual treasure chest of adult toys, some of which even eluded her rather broad knowledge. She quickly looked away, not eager to point out that particular asset of the suite.

"Watch this." She found the panel on the side of the sleek bedside table and pushed a button. In front of the chandelier, facing the detailed headboard, a slim screen lowered from a hidden recess in the ceiling. "Plasma. Awesome, isn't it?"

Jack smiled and moved beside her to look at the panel. "What do the rest of these buttons do?"

His shoulder brushed hers, his faint woodsy scent so intoxicating, it took her a second to regain her senses. "Uh, lots of things." She cursed herself for the inane comment. "Everything in the suite is controlled from here—the television, of course, the temperature, the drapes, the sound system, the lights…"

"Impressive."

"You don't sound impressed."

He smiled again, and she realized that he probably already had a plasma TV, a comparable sound system, everything he needed at his fingertips. And if he didn't, it wasn't because he couldn't afford it.

"Ah, well, it beats having to slap the side of my ten-year-old twenty-inch to clear the reception." She sighed. "So what do you think? Good backdrop, huh?"

His gaze narrowed, he surveyed the room. "Anything else in here I should know about?"

"Such as?"

His frown deepened, lingering on the armoire. "This hotel is known for more than its luxurious rooms."

"Oh, you mean the sex stuff." She grinned at his grimace. "I didn't think you were interested."

"I'm not." He gave her a long stern look. Which didn't faze her. He had the most incredible hazel eyes. She could stare into them all night. "I don't like surprises."

"I totally get it. No surprises."

"I have your word."

She tried not to laugh. "Yes."

He glanced at his watch. "Today's Wednesday, when do you want to start shooting?"

"Saturday?" She noticed his hesitation and quickly added, "Whatever suits your schedule. I know you don't do the weekend shows so I figured—"

"You watch my show?" Amusement gleamed in his eyes.

"Of course. Doesn't everyone?" Too perky. He had to know she was lying.

He smiled. "I'll have to check my calendar to confirm Saturday, but I think that'll work."

"Great."

They both moved toward the door. "My driver will be here at any minute," he said.

She got nervous all of a sudden. Kind of a warm flash heated her face. Clammy hands. Just like when she'd waited for more than two hours for her one-and-only prom date. The bastard never showed. Her mom had spent half their rent on the stupid pink dress and rose boutonniere for nothing.

"You have my number?" she asked, annoyed that her voice sounded too high. "To confirm Saturday?"

"I do. What time did you want to get started?"

Before opening the double doors, she glanced over her shoulder to make sure they'd left the suite the way they'd found it. "The earlier the better."

"Seven?"

"Terrific."

"How long do you think it'll take?"

"Hard to tell." She closed the door behind them and then checked the doorknob to make sure it was locked. "Depends on how— What?"

He was trying to hide a smile but doing a poor job of it. "Nothing. You were saying…"

She stopped and frowned at him. "Come on. What?"

He absently shook his head. "You remind me of my sister. She always has to check the doors and stove twice before leaving the house."

"I checked it once. That doesn't make me neurotic,"

she said, not sure which annoyed her more, the neurosis implication or being likened to his sister.

"I never accused you of being neurotic. Now if you always get a block away from your apartment and have to keep going back—"

"I did that only one time," she blurted before she censored herself, and then as she turned back toward the elevator, muttered, "I thought I'd left the iron on."

He laughed. "Didn't mean to strike a nerve."

"You didn't." As soon as she depressed the down button, the elevator doors opened and they stepped inside. He stood close, closer than was necessary in the empty car.

She breathed in slowly and deeply, tried to exhale without making too much noise, and stared straight ahead at the doors. His nearness meant nothing, of course. It wasn't deliberate on his part, more an absence of thought. That certain knowledge didn't stop her pulse from accelerating or her mouth from going totally dry.

Jack said nothing during the ride down to the lobby. Which suited Madison just fine. She didn't trust herself to speak. Anyway, his thoughts had probably already strayed to whichever nubile young starlet he was meeting for dinner tonight.

Over the past couple of years he'd been linked to a number of actresses and models, from New York to Sweden. Nothing had seriously developed. As far as she knew. Obviously he subscribed to the variety-is-the-spice-of-life philosophy. But then again, who in their right mind believed the tabloids.

The doors opened to the lobby and its lush expanse of sea-foam-green carpeting, and he asked, "Need a ride?"

"Thanks, but I'm going the other way."

His lips twitched. "How do you know where I'm going?" He put on his coat.

She sighed and turned up her collar in anticipation of the chilly fall air. "I like to walk or take the subway."

"It's cold out there."

"I know." She stopped at the front desk and dropped off the key. "Cold, dark and full of surprises."

He looked warily at her as if she'd really creeped him out.

Grinning, she buttoned her blazer as they made their way to the door. "Good surprises, that make me want to stop and whip out my camera. The kind you miss when you're riding in a car."

"Right."

She offered her hand. "I look forward to working with you, Jack."

"Me, too."

"Liar." Laughing, she turned up her collar and headed home.

JACK SLID INTO THE BACKSEAT and leaned against the leather upholstery, watching her stride along Forty-sixth. No jacket, just her thin coat, even though it had to be only forty degrees.

"Where to, boss?" Dutch looked at him in the rear-view mirror. "Your apartment?"

"Yeah, I guess so." He'd have dinner, something disgustingly healthy his housekeeper had left in the refrigerator for him. Then watch some boring television. "Dutch, I've changed my mind."

The young man's eyes instantly met his. "Okay," he

said, disappointment in his voice. Probably thought his day wouldn't be over yet. "Where to?"

"Drop me at the studio, and then go home."

"But how will—"

"I think I remember how to hail a cab." Hell, maybe he'd even walk the three miles and skip the treadmill tomorrow morning.

"But, boss—"

"Dutch, don't argue."

The man said nothing, only frowned and then concentrated on pulling the black Lincoln Town Car away from the curb and into traffic.

Jack sighed. He hadn't meant to sound short. "So how are Jenny and the kids these days?"

"Noisy and expensive." Dutch snorted. "The three of them are gonna land me in the poor house."

Jack smiled. He'd known the man for five years, and the litany had been the same. But everyone who knew him also knew he lived and breathed for his family.

"Yep, don't ever have girls, boss. Too high maintenance. I ought to send them to Catholic school. Make 'em wear uniforms. No more whining for designer jeans."

"I doubt that would stop them. Well, maybe when they're forty."

"I won't care then. They'll be somebody else's problem."

Jack chuckled, his gaze lingering in Madison's direction, but she'd already disappeared. Laying his head back, he briefly closed his eyes.

Saturday was going to be hell. Why had he ever agreed to this absurdity? How could people regard him as a serious newsman with his face spread across the pages of a magazine? He understood why so many celebrities had to accept that kind of exposure. They had to promote their new movies and themselves. He'd interviewed enough of them himself. Most of them didn't like to do it, but they understood that the hype was part of the business.

He didn't fall into that category. He just investigated and reported the news. Not that he did half the amount of investigation he'd like. His main job was to look good in front of the camera each morning, banter with his cohost and, yeah, subtly flirt with his female audience. He knew all that, and he'd played the game. But it was getting old. Fast.

Sighing, he brought his head up and pinched the bridge of his nose. His temples were starting to throb. Probably from the scotch. He didn't drink often and generally not on an empty stomach. He should've offered to buy Madison dinner. Better than going back to his apartment and eating alone. Just like he did most nights. Something he normally preferred.

Not tonight, though.

He looked out the heavily tinted window and watched two young women chatting as they walked, one of them tugging at the leash of a black Great Dane, who seemed hell-bent on stopping at every trash receptacle and tree. Other pedestrians gave them a wide berth, dodging out of the way when the dog started sniffing too intimately.

Jack smiled. He didn't see many big dogs in the city. People mostly kept smaller dogs, which made sense because of the size of the average apartment. Small. Really small. He'd had one of those once. In the beginning, before he'd taken over the morning show. The bedroom and living room practically shared the same space, yet had escaped the label of studio apartment. But at least it hadn't been a walk-up, and a doorman always monitored the building's entrance.

Now, everything was different. He had a large, well-appointed three-story brownstone, a housekeeper who spoiled him and a house in Connecticut on the water. He even had Dutch to drive him wherever he wanted to go. So why wasn't he happy? Hell, he knew why: he missed being out in the field. But was he really ready to give all this up?

4

"SORRY I'M LATE." Madison flew through the doors of Shelly's Family Portraits and dropped her bag behind the counter next to Shelly, who stared at the new computer she'd bought last week. "I'll be set up before the Dennisons get here."

"Don't rush. They're gonna be late," Shelly said without looking away from the computer screen. "Mrs. Dennison called ten minutes ago. Oh, and she changed her mind about the blue-sky backdrop."

"Oh, God, what does she want now?"

"The garden scene. The one with the butterflies." Shelly pressed a button and then muttered a mild curse. "Hey, do you know anything about these damn contraptions?"

"A little but let me get set up first." Madison barely got the words out through clenched teeth as she headed into the cramped back room.

The butterfly scene. How she hated that one. In fact, she hated every one of the cheesy backdrops. She'd begged Shelly to let her take the clients to Central Park. She'd be able to get some dynamite shots there. But Shelly was old school. Claimed no one wanted to be dragged outdoors when there were perfectly good fake backgrounds right in the studio.

At least Shelly was an easygoing boss. She required little of Madison, letting her work sporadically when she needed money, unless Shelly got slammed with appointments, which didn't happen often. Madison just had to remember this was only part-time and temporary. Some easy money to help make ends meet. And then let it go. She'd absolutely die if she thought she had to take family portraits for the rest of her life.

But not after she made the cover of *Today's Man*. If she hadn't been confident before she'd met Jack Logan in the flesh, she would be now. He was the perfect subject. She couldn't think of anyone she'd rather photograph more than him. The strong line of his jaw alone was enough to make a woman weep. And those hazel eyes, caught by the right light, seemed to glitter with deviltry, daring and tempting and mocking every feminine resolve.

Good thing she was immune. Not counting the dream she'd had two nights ago where she practically tore off his clothes. The brief memory brought a flash of heat, and she accidentally kicked the tripod. She caught it before it went over but not without causing a racket.

"You okay back there?" Shelly had lost most of her southern drawl except when it suited her purpose, but her trademark blond "big" hair hadn't changed since she'd moved to New York fifteen years ago, a former Texas beauty queen, with more hope than promise.

"Fine. I'm almost done." Madison smoothed the horrid butterfly backdrop and tacked the right corner. "Which one of the darling little Dennisons am I shooting today?"

"Oops. Should've warned you. It's the twins."

Madison groaned and pulled out another chair. Of the four kids, the twins were the ones who made her most insane. At only three years old the boys were already tyrants, but their mother considered them simply adorable. Bad combination.

"I know they irritate you," Shelly said, lowering her voice as she ducked into the back, "but frankly, if Eileen Dennison weren't so neurotic about capturing every little pout and smile, I'm not sure I would've made the rent last month."

Madison got it. It was Shelly's subtle way of telling her to make nice with Eileen Dennison, who, Madison had to admit, was great for business. Paid cash, too.

"Don't worry," Madison said as she bent down to peer through the lens at the backdrop. "I'll treat the little monsters like royalty."

Shelly chuckled. "You're especially good with the little ones. Mothers ask for you a lot."

"Yeah, well not without a great deal of effort." She straightened, satisfied with the angle of the camera.

"I was thinking that maybe when I get better at that computer I can make some flyers. Pay some kid to hand them out at the corner." Shelly pulled a tube of lipstick out of her pants pocket and used the mirror on the far wall to apply bright red to her lips. "Might be able to drum us up some more business. What do you think?"

Madison hesitated. She wouldn't be here much longer. Shelly knew that. Madison had been up-front from the beginning. "Maybe."

"Yeah, I know. You won't be doing this much longer." Shelly turned to her and shrugged. "I figure when the time comes that you kick me to the curb I'll find some fresh graduate from NYU with gobs of student loans to repay and in desperate need of money."

"Excuse me? Kick you to the curb?"

Shelly laughed. "I'm just so jealous I could spit. Tell me about him."

"Jack Logan?"

"Who else do you think I mean?" Shelly planted her hands on her curvy hips. "I've been dying to hear about your meeting for two days. When's the shoot? Tell me everything."

Madison grinned. "He's gorgeous. Breathtaking. What more can I say?"

"Girl, I can turn on the TV and see that for myself. I want to hear the juicy stuff."

"We had a business meeting, for goodness sakes."

"So? I heard he's quite the flirt."

Madison shook her head and made another adjustment to the tripod. "First, the only place you could have 'heard' anything is from one of those ridiculous tabloids you read. Second, I'm hardly in Jack Logan's league."

"Well, Miss Know-It-All, there's a whole lot more truth in those magazines than you think. They can't just pull those things out of thin air."

"Of course not."

Shelly chuckled. "You're no fun."

"You haven't seen me after two margaritas." Madison checked her watch. "What time are they supposed to get here?"

"Any minute." Shelly poked her head out front, even though a warning buzzer went off every time someone came through the door, and then she looked back at

Madison. "Evidently, he isn't very tall, and he has to wear elevated shoes."

"I'm five-eight and he has a good five inches on me. Strike one for evidently."

Shelly snorted. "Is it true he's dating Charlize Theron?"

"I wouldn't have the faintest idea."

"Last year he dumped that soap actress without warning. You shoulda seen the picture of her bawling her poor red eyes out."

"You of all people, Shelly Mayfield."

"What?"

"Like you don't know how pictures can be altered."

Shelly shrugged. "That doesn't mean the sad thing wasn't mooning after him."

"I give up." Shaking her head, Madison brushed past Shelly and headed to the front of the studio. The place was tiny and she'd be stuck in back with the Dennison twins and their doting mother long enough.

Shelly followed, continuing to babble, the list of women Jack had been seeing growing longer. Madison tried to shut her out. She didn't care about Jack's exploits. In fact, she didn't want to think about them at all. Likely none of it was true, and she worked better when she liked her subject.

The door buzzer sounded and in came the Dennisons.

"I don't wanna take my picture. I wanna go to the park."

Mrs. Dennison had the red-faced boy by the collar. The other towheaded twin meekly held her hand. "Toby, we'll go to the park when we're through. And we'll have hot dogs and ice cream, okay?"

"No, I wanna go now." He started crying, wailing really. Loud enough for everyone in Queens to hear him.

Mrs. Dennison smiled brightly at Madison. "We're here."

Madison's head started to ache. She couldn't wait for tomorrow. Oh, yeah. And if she didn't get that man to take his shirt off, she'd take the Dennison twins to a whole day at the park.

JACK FOUND A KEY CARD waiting for him at the front desk, just as Madison's message had indicated. He used it to take the elevator to the rooftop garden where she said they should meet. Listening to the voice mail last night had brought some relief. He'd dreaded today since the moment he met her. Nothing personal. It was the whole sexiest-man nonsense. But the garden was at least a public spot and as good a start as any in the hotel.

Still, he wasn't fooling himself. Eventually, she'd try to cajole him into taking off his shirt, getting into the pool, or lounging on one of the beds in the suite. Photographers were all alike. The more tantalizing or incriminating the shot, the better they liked it.

He didn't begrudge her making a living. In fact, he was in awe of some photographers, the way they could evoke the deepest emotion with a single shot, one that could galvanize an entire city to action. Without a doubt great things had been accomplished through photography. None of which involved celebrity photos.

The elevator doors opened and the scent of gardenias greeted him before he got out. Still early, not quite seven, the garden appeared deserted. And then he saw her. By the gazebo, a half-eaten doughnut in one hand, while she used her other hand to fiddle with the camera mounted on a tripod.

Glad she hadn't seen him yet, his gaze went to the red sweater she wore, the sleeves pushed up and the fabric molding nice high breasts. Not too large. Perfect for her slim build.

She took a hearty bite of the doughnut, and then enthusiastically licked her lips. He smiled but then pulled a straight face before noisily clearing his throat.

She turned to him with a look of surprise, still chewing, and then glanced at her watch. "Wow! It's almost seven."

"How long have you been here?"

"About an hour." She gestured to a small silver thermos. "Want some coffee?"

"Later maybe."

Her gaze went to his leather garment bag. "Are those the shirts?"

"Yes, ma'am, one white, one black, both long-sleeved, just as you ordered."

"I requested."

"I stand corrected."

Her lips curved. "Want a doughnut before we get started? I've got glazed and buttermilk."

"I'll pass."

She took another bite, this one smaller than her last one, her gaze going to an alcove where a white stone bench had been nestled between two hibiscus bushes boasting large orange blossoms. "In about fifteen minutes the lighting will be perfect in that corner. What do you think of taking a few shots there?"

"I don't know." He had nothing against flowers, but the setting was... "Doesn't it look a little feminine?"

She thoughtfully pursed her lips for a second. "I

know quite a few gay guys who subscribe to *Today's Man*. We should really appeal to all readers."

He stared at her, unable to tell if she were serious. "The gays I know aren't feminine."

"I was only joking." She cocked her head to the side and studied him for a moment, something that looked like approval gleamed in her eyes. "But that was an excellent answer."

"Happy I passed the test. Now I can get some sleep tonight."

She laughed, took the last bite of her doughnut and then wiped her hands with a paper napkin. A speck of glaze clung to her lower lip, and he waited for her to wipe her mouth. But she wadded up the napkin and stuffed it into a white paper sack.

"Okay, I'm going to start taking some candid shots to get us both loosened up." She picked up a camera and met his eyes. "Something wrong?"

"No," he said, his gaze automatically going back to her mouth before he caught himself and walked away. "Any particular place you want me?"

"Nope."

He turned around and a flash went off. Startled, he blinked and stepped back.

"Perfect," she said, and snapped another photo. "Just walk around, look at the flowers, whatever."

Another flash. And then another.

He pushed a hand through his hair, tried to relax. Tried not to dwell on the fact he'd rather be just about anywhere else on the planet but here.

She lowered the camera and stared glumly at him. "Can you at least try not to look as if you're at a funeral?"

"I wasn't prepared for you to start shooting."

"This is just an exercise. None of it counts. Pretend I'm not even here."

"Right." The glaze stubbornly clung to her lower lip. He ought to tell her. If nothing else, just so he could quit obsessing. Quit fixating on her mouth. She'd get the wrong idea. Though she did have nice lips. Perfectly shaped. Naturally full without a collagen overdose.

"Terrific." Another flash. "That's the look I want."

He dragged his gaze away from her mouth and turned his head.

"Hey, come on, you were doing great." She frowned at him over the camera. "What's wrong?"

"I wasn't prepared."

"That was the point. You know…candid." She smiled and then peered through the lens again. "You'd rather prepare? Then whatever it was you were thinking, do it again."

Jack took a deep breath. This woman was going to make him nuts. "I think I need some of that coffee now."

"Sure. Help yourself."

She kept snapping away as he walked to the thermos. The top that served as a cup was there, empty, but obviously having been used. He looked around but didn't see any others.

"Oh, damn." She lowered the camera. "I forgot to bring an extra cup. I'll run downstairs and borrow one from the restaurant."

"No need." He didn't actually care about coffee. It had been more to distract himself from her mouth. "Later."

"Really." She laid down the camera. "It'll only take a minute."

"Madison?" He touched her arm, his fingertips grazing the skin that was bared below the sleeve. "Forget the coffee."

Her lips parted in surprise, and he stared at the minuscule fleck of white that shouldn't have mattered.

"Okay," she said slowly, her arm tensing beneath his touch. "We'll go ahead and get started."

"Good idea." He lowered his hand, but the awkwardness clung heavily to the air between them.

She hesitated, looking uncertain, adding to his regret. And then she suddenly stepped back, raised the camera and clicked. "Perfect."

He blinked and jerked back.

"Sorry, didn't mean to startle you." She turned to the white bench and stared at it for a moment. "You know what…forget the bench. How about standing over there?"

She moved briskly to a small clearing that created access to the point where the wall met the glass dome. Beyond was a partial city view painted a golden orange from the rising sun.

"Right here is great." She gestured excitedly. "But we'll have to move fast."

He understood the limited window of opportunity and quickly complied. She was all business as she prodded him into place, instructing him to turn his head one way and then the other, to angle his shoulders in different positions. For the next five minutes she focused and clicked—it felt like a hundred times. And then she stopped, lowered the camera and frowned.

"This isn't working."

Anger ignited in his gut but he kept it at bay because she looked genuinely disappointed. "Why not?"

"You're too stiff."

"I've done exactly what you've told me to do."

She nodded absently as if she weren't really listening, an experience foreign to him. He didn't like being ignored. "Let's go back to candid shots," she said finally. "Forget that I'm here. Just do whatever you'd do if you were by yourself."

"Right."

"Work with me here, would you?" She cocked her head to look past him. "We're gonna lose the sun in about five minutes."

"Hmm…usually comes up about this time."

"Very funny," she said, and clicked. "Perfect. Keep up the wisecracks. Think about the last joke you heard, about your date last weekend. Think about getting laid."

That startled a laugh out of him.

She kept clicking. "Not the response I expected, but good. Keep going."

Jack shook his head. She was something all right. Not like the women he'd met in the past few years. The ones who were either absurdly star struck or slyly using him to chase fame themselves.

No questioning Madison's ambition, and that was okay, admirable actually. She was up-front about what she wanted. Her interest in him was clearly business, which allowed him to relax. Not that he agreed with the direction in which she wanted to take this photo shoot, but he understood it was her job to try. It was his to set boundaries.

"I'm losing you," she said impatiently before snapping a couple more shots and then lowering the camera. "When I think about getting laid, I'm sure I look a whole lot more excited than deciding what to get for dinner."

He smiled. "Give me an example."

"What?"

"Go ahead. Show me how I'm supposed to look."

"We're wasting time." She raised the camera to eye level again, but couldn't quite hide the smile tugging at her mouth.

"I'm serious. Show me how *you'd* look."

"Hell, I'm not going for disbelief." She sighed and brought the camera down. "It doesn't matter. We've lost the sun."

He watched her turn around and tinker with the tripod, and wondered what she'd meant by disbelief. He sometimes overheard the women at the studio complaining about how difficult it was to meet a decent guy in the city. Although someone as attractive and smart and ambitious as Madison shouldn't have a problem.

She wasn't drop-dead gorgeous nor did she possess any particular feature that would earn her a spot in front of the camera, but she had a casual sexiness that appealed to him. Serious, intelligent eyes, which sparkled when that wide, generous mouth curved into a smile, was a big draw for him. Long legs didn't hurt. He had a thing for them, and she fit well into that category, too.

"Look, I'm sorry if I ruined your shot," he said before he knew what he was going to say.

She turned and studied him for a moment and then quickly focused the camera and clicked twice. "That works."

"What? Me looking humble?"

"You humble?" She chuckled. "Right."

"Hey, I resent that."

She focused and clicked again. And again as she stepped closer. "Now we're talking."

He had to laugh. "Does anything faze you?"

"Not much." She looped the camera strap around her neck and let the camera rest over her breasts.

Whether from stimulation from the camera or the cool air, her nipples strained against her T-shirt, a set of pearls that captivated his attention and sent heat to his groin. He quickly looked away.

"How about we try over here again?" She gestured toward the white stone bench, and he readily complied, giving her his back as he moved in that direction.

In fact, he welcomed the distraction. It was going to be a long day, and the last thing they needed was an inappropriate look making them both uncomfortable.

"Right here would be good," she said, suddenly so close behind him he could smell her citrus-scented shampoo.

Unable to resist, he inhaled deeply, and then when he turned, she was right there. Inches away, her minty breath warm on his chin.

"Sorry," she muttered, and quickly moved back, except her breast brushed his arm. "I didn't mean to crowd you."

"No problem." He lied. His slacks felt uncomfortably tight.

He didn't dare look down.

5

JACK WATCHED HER STUDY the trellis of small pink roses that flanked the left side of the bench. He didn't think it was a matter of trying to avoid him. Fortunately she seemed oblivious to the contact and genuinely interested in rearranging one of the vines so that a spray of roses cascaded over the bench.

He took a couple of deep breaths. Told himself how ridiculous it was to have reacted, and everything started to settle down.

Except her nipple had responded to the pressure of his arm, and it required all his effort not to stare at the persistent nub.

"There." She gingerly released the vine, and stepped back. "Perfect."

"Okay."

She looked over at him almost as if she'd forgotten he was there. "I'm trying to set a certain mood, get a certain look." She frowned. "What would you do if you were planning a romantic date?"

"Romantic?"

"Yes, romantic. You know, out of the ordinary, something that bares your soul to someone special who you want to impress." She briefly closed her eyes and gave her head an emphatic shake. "No, not impress. She's someone you care about…you've never felt this way about a woman before. You want to show her how you feel with every detail that you've planned for this date."

"Romantic." He sighed. Not exactly his style. "Right."

"Stretch your imagination a little," she said flatly, which made him smile.

"Help me out here."

She squinted at him. "The longer you fool around, the longer this is gonna take."

"Who's fooling around? I usually take a woman to dinner and the theater. I'm a boring date. Now you know. Okay?"

She grinned. "You are a boring date. But so am I, so don't be insulted." She sobered, straightened and briefly closed her eyes. "Together we can do this. Okay. Imagine that you've planned a sunrise picnic. Up here." She gestured toward the roses and bush of fragrant yellow flowers he didn't recognize.

"You've brought candles and champagne and chocolate-covered strawberries, soft romantic music and— What?"

"Nothing. Go on."

"You look highly amused."

He cleared his throat. "I'm just listening. You're really very good at this."

"Obviously that isn't your idea of a romantic date. That's fine." She stepped back, eyed him for a moment. "Forget the romantic part. Let's go back to you getting laid."

He laughed.

"Consider the picnic foreplay." She raised the camera again and focused. "You've been waiting for this moment for a month. Come on, let your imagination run with it. You're expecting to have the best sex of your life."

He started laughing and she glared at him over the camera.

"Not exactly what I was looking for," she said dryly.

"You don't see the humor in this?"

She blew out a puff of air. "Let's try this again. No laughing."

"No, ma'am."

"I'm serious, Logan."

"Me, too. Look. Not even a smile."

She shook her head in admonishment, but her lips curved slightly. "Ready?"

He sighed. This was absurd. What a waste of a Saturday. He could have been golfing in Myrtle Beach. Hell, a trip to the dentist would've been more productive. Certainly easier.

She repositioned the camera and when the strap around her neck went up, so did her T-shirt, exposing a strip of pale skin above the waistband of her jeans. Something gold and dangly caught his eye. A ring with some kind of charm gleamed from her navel.

His gaze traveled up to the hem of her T-shirt. Another three inches and it would ride the swell of her breasts. His gut tightened. He wanted to see more.

"Great."

He heard her voice, heard the camera click. Neither of which hampered his wildly inappropriate thoughts.

"Okay," she said, moving back and taking one shot

after another. "Whatever you're thinking, keep thinking it. This is awesome stuff."

Her permission was mere formality. His imagination had already taken over, and he wondered what it would feel like to tongue her navel, tease it and her piercing with his teeth. He wondered if she had any more, in more-intimate places.

The hell of it was that he didn't go in for that kind of thing, and Madison hadn't seemed the type who would, either. The incongruity was what fascinated him most.

That was a lie. His gaze lowered to her thighs, to that narrow place where they didn't meet.

Her long lean legs interested him far more. Her generous derriere sparked more than a little interest, as well. As slender as she was, her backside was nice and round and entirely too tempting.

His hands reflexively fisted and he imagined his arms wrapped around her, his hands kneading firm flesh while her naked breasts pressed against his bare chest. He'd lift her easily so that her legs could wrap around his waist.

He bet she'd be incredible. Totally open and uninhibited. Eager to please and be pleased.

His groin tightened.

He tried to stop. He had to look away or end up embarrassing the hell out of himself.

MADISON TOOK SEVERAL dozen shots in rapid succession. This was great stuff. Fabulous. He was finally getting in the spirit of the shoot. The thought had no sooner formed in her head when he tensed and twisted away from her.

"Work with me here," she said, and snapped a couple more she knew she wouldn't use, but unwilling to interrupt the flow while waiting for him to relax.

He briefly closed his eyes and with what seemed to be an inordinate amount of effort, gave her his attention again.

"That's it. Look at the camera," she said. "Love it. Make it your best friend. Tell it your secrets."

Letting out a grunt, he hunched his shoulders and rested his elbows on his bent knees.

"Okay," she said, lowering the camera. "Wanna tell me what's going on?"

A pained look creased his face. "I think I need that coffee now."

"Now?"

"Uh, yeah." He didn't make a move to get up.

"All right." She hesitated. "I'll run downstairs for a clean cup."

"Thanks."

Setting down her camera, she slid him another look. He kept his gaze averted, his body still bent over, kind of the way she ended up last Saturday after eating too many cocktail wienies.

Heck, she didn't get it. One minute he was cooperative and looking as if he were about to pull an all-nighter with the blond supermodel du jour. And now, he looked as if he were about to expire.

She got to the elevator, pressed the down button. This was crazy. They were wasting time. "I have a better idea," she said turning back to him. "Let's move to—"

He'd just gotten to his feet.

Her breath caught in her throat and she tried unsuccessfully to swallow, tried not to stare at the unmistakable bulge straining against his fly.

Focusing on his face didn't help.

Awareness smoldered in his darkened hazel eyes, holding her gaze, possessing it for one incredible moment before he glanced away. "You were saying?"

His voice was even, composed, unlike the tornado going through her insides. Her mouth had gone dry, and words stuck in her throat. Even though she knew his arousal had nothing to do with her. Hell, she'd provoked him into creating the sexy private images in his head. God knew which model or actress had stirred that kind of raw desire.

Damn, she should have gotten a shot of that last look.

Madison replied, "I think we've gotten enough shots up here. Why don't we move to the Haiku Suite and have coffee there?"

"Fine."

"All right then." She headed back toward her equipment and gathered her bag and camera, willing her hands to quit shaking. Nothing horribly noticeable, but enough of a tremor to make her clumsy and she nearly knocked over the tripod.

Thankfully he grabbed it and proceeded to carry the tripod toward the elevator. The fact he carried it as if it were a shield nearly sent her into a fit of nervous giggles.

She took a couple of deep breaths. The really cleansing kind she'd learned from Talia that went straight to the diaphragm. The exercise calmed her somewhat. As long as she kept her thoughts on business. Unfortunately, that included Jack Logan.

By THE TIME THEY GOT to the suite it was only eight-thirty and Jack was already thinking about calling it quits for the day. It was all his fault things were going badly. What the hell was he thinking fantasizing about her? Picturing her naked. Wondering if she was a Brazilian wax kind of woman, or if she went au naturel.

Damn it.

He concentrated on the suite's interesting decor. An Asian theme with silk upholstered walls, black lacquer furniture and very expensive-looking Oriental rugs. He hadn't seen this particular suite before, not at the opening and not with Madison earlier in the week.

Hopefully this change of venue didn't mean anything. He ducked his head into the bedroom and spotted the notorious armoire. Or should he say toy chest. Piper had referred to it that way at the opening, and since it was her hotel, she should know. Each room had one for the more adventurous guests, along with a selection of adult videos. Not his thing. But he wasn't a prude about it, either. He just hoped Madison didn't have any unpleasant surprises planned.

"Something wrong?" She set down her equipment and closed the door behind her, her concerned gaze narrowed on him.

He rolled his right shoulder trying to release the tension building around his neck. "We didn't see this suite the other day."

"No, but my first choice is booked. This isn't bad, though, huh? Really more masculine." She glanced around with an analytical eye, and his gaze headed straight for her rounded backside.

"I'll call room service for some coffee," he muttered and focused on finding a phone.

"No, wait." She moistened her lips. "It won't take me but a minute to run downstairs."

"Seems like a waste of time."

She grimaced. "The thing is, I didn't make arrangements for any type of billing. And since we aren't registered guests…"

"I'll take care of it." Ignoring her protests, he found a phone and quickly arranged for a pot of their strongest brew. He'd probably regret the caffeine, although he'd developed some immunity thanks to the nasty habit of downing an entire pot each morning while prepping for his show.

Madison gave him a wry look.

He shrugged. "Celebrity does have its privileges. I didn't make the rules."

"I'm not being critical." She smiled. "Envious maybe."

"Yeah, well, it's definitely a trade-off."

"Guess there's a lot of schlock that goes with the job, huh?"

He smiled back. "That's one way of putting it."

"Still wouldn't mind giving it a shot." She shrugged and carefully set her camera next to a vase of fresh flowers. "I'd like to take a roll or two of film in here, and then some in the bedroom."

"Why?"

"It's part of the suite."

"Funny."

"Come on." She grinned. "Loosen up."

"Remember our deal."

"Deal?" She faked a perplexed frown, and then tried to hide a smile as she opened the silk drapes, letting in the sunlight. She turned around to study the effect on the room, and nearly caught him eyeing the way the soft denim clung to her rear.

"I'll give you the benefit of the doubt and assume you know what I'm talking about."

Ignoring him, she trailed her hand lightly over the sleek black lacquer sofa table, all the more impressive bathed in sunlight. "Oh, my, can you imagine staying here for real? Well, I guess you could. Us peons only get to see a room like this in the movies."

He let the remark slide even though he disliked the class reference. "It's okay. But I've stayed in better places."

"Where's that?"

"Out in the open. Under the stars. Air so clean and pure you're not sure how to breathe it."

"Whoa. Obviously you're the outdoor type, but I didn't know you were that gung-ho."

"I'm not talking about recreational camping. Being in the field is the real rush. Hot sand under your body while you sleep. But you only close your eyes for a few minutes at a time." He walked to the entertainment center, found a remote and stepped back to turn on the television—a flat-panel LCD much like the one he had in his own bedroom. After flipping through a couple of channels, he found CNN and then muted the sound.

"Sleeping only a few minutes at a time doesn't sound like fun." She stared at the screen, grimacing at the graphic coverage of yet another bombing in the Middle East.

"Ever work out in the field, Madison?"

"Does Times Square count?"

He smiled, but kept his somber gaze on the action on the screen. "If you get the chance, take an assignment abroad. The experience will be unforgettable. You owe that to yourself."

"Um, I'm not really that kind of photographer. Anyway, I'm not big on sleeping outdoors."

"Trust me. You wouldn't care about how hard the ground is or how good a lobster tail drowned in butter might sound. It won't matter how far away you are from civilization. Adrenaline takes over. It simmers in your veins. You have no concept of time. Days, weeks, months, it doesn't matter."

The curious way she studied him effectively shut him up. He'd said too much. His attention went back to the television, and a second before he switched off the remote she snapped a picture.

He jerked back. "What are you doing?"

"That was incredible. That was—" She slowly shook her head, her expression almost reverent. "You're gonna love that shot. It's totally you."

"You don't even know me."

She blinked. "Granted, but I listened to what you just said, and that picture captured it. The passion in your words, in your voice. It was truth." She cocked her head to the side. "You obviously miss being out there—getting the story. Why aren't you out there more?"

"More?" He laughed. "I haven't done any field reporting since I accepted the anchor seat." Of course the network brass would disagree. Except their idea of field reporting was doing the morning show live from a movie set.

"Why not?"

He hesitated. "It's not feasible." Was she really that naive? "Shouldn't we get started?"

"Right." She looked as if she wanted to say something more but wisely turned away. "Let's see…the couch. Or maybe…" She moved back slowly, while studying the room. "Over here." She gestured for him to sit on a fabulous green suede chair.

He did, but she frowned and shook her head.

"That's not right. Let's try the couch again."

He sighed, got to his feet and moved to the couch.

"Okay, good, but can you just kind of turn this way." She angled her body by example, the T-shirt molding her breasts and blowing his concentration. "More like this." She touched his shoulder and positioned him toward the window.

He kept his gaze straight ahead; if he turned even a little, her breast would be far too close to his lips.

"Look this way a little," she said, and when he hesitated, she touched the side of his jaw, a light, innocent touch that shouldn't have held such potency.

Her fingers quickly fell away, and he wondered if she'd shared the same heated reaction. Crazy as it was. Not just crazy. Full-blown insane. He never mixed business with pleasure. Anyway, he didn't have brief flings. Too messy. Fodder for the tabloids.

"Um, could you just kind of face the window a little more?" She'd stepped back, her hands at her sides.

"Like this?"

"A little more." She started to show him and then lowered her hands again. "Don't look directly into the sun but enough that it lights your face."

He smiled. "And spotlight all my imperfections?"

She snorted. "If you have one, I haven't found it yet."

Rarely did he get embarrassed but that did it. "Trust me. They're there."

She grinned and got up close. "Now I'm curious."

For a foolish second he thought she was going to kiss him, but then she used her index finger to nudge up his chin.

"There." She moved back and looked through the camera lens. "Put your arm along the back of the couch. But keep your—"

He looked over at her.

"...chin angled." Sighing, she lowered the camera. "Maybe we'd better stick to candid shots for a while."

"Look, I know how to follow camera direction." He pointedly looked at his watch. "Just tell me what you want me to do."

Annoyance flickered in her eyes. "Excuse me, I thought I'd made myself perfectly clear."

He rubbed the back of his neck, regretting having taken out his edginess on her. She was just trying to do her job. "I didn't mean to sound impatient."

"I wasn't exactly grace personified." She lifted the camera from around her neck, and his gaze went to the hem of her T-shirt. A flash of bare skin but that was it. "We jumped into this pretty hard. The coffee should be here any minute. Let's have some, talk about what we'd like to accomplish today and then get back to work."

"Good idea," he said. Maybe he'd ask her about the navel ring, or whatever it was. Then again, too personal.

She took the other side of the couch and started to draw her legs up but stopped before her sneakers hit the fabric. "Oh, boy, that's all I'd need. It would probably take two month's salary just to dry clean this sucker."

Jack glanced around at the tasteful furnishings, the Oriental rug under their feet. "This is a Zang Toi design, isn't it?"

"You're asking me?" She laughed. "Bloomingdales is still high end to me."

"I confess. I vaguely remember the name coming up at the grand opening. I don't even know if Zang Toi is a man or a woman."

Her smile said she didn't believe him. "It's okay. It's not your fault you're an elitist." Her smile widened. "You didn't make the rules."

"Hey, I'm just a farm boy from Nebraska."

She looked serious all of a sudden. "Maybe we should play that up."

"What?"

"Your leap from humble beginnings to stardom and international fame."

"There was no leap." He glanced at his watch. Where the hell was that coffee? "I worked hard to get to where I am."

"I wasn't implying you hadn't. So leap is the wrong word. I only meant that we should play up that theme, or journey, if you will. After all, farms boys are sexy, too."

"Hell, there you go again."

"Come on. Sex sells and I sure as hell didn't make that rule. Hey." She stretched out her leg and with the toe of her sneaker nudged his foot. "I'm not gonna go crazy with this shoot. I promised it would be tasteful and I meant it."

The contact was friendly and innocent enough but when their eyes met he felt a disturbing pull in his groin that had him shifting positions. She blinked and shifted, too, so that her leg was well out of reach. "Tell me how you went from Nebraska to the Gulf War."

"I'd just graduated from college and the station where I'd interned the previous summer offered me a job."

"And they sent you to the Gulf? Just like that?"

"Hardly." He smiled. "I actually had plans to head for New York but my dad had passed away the same year and I figured I'd better stick close to home. Pure dumb luck because at the last minute they needed a flunky to accompany their overseas reporter. When he got sick over there, I was thrown in front of the camera."

She grinned, forming a tiny dimple he hadn't noticed before. "Not exactly close to home."

"Nope, but the family really pushed for me to take advantage of the opportunity." He'd been young and full of himself and hadn't argued when maybe he should have, but everything turned out fine and he tried not to think about that.

"So, letters from your fan club started pouring in and soon you were a permanent fixture."

He cringed at the accuracy. His popularity with the female audience had pretty much launched his career. Not that he hadn't been a damn good reporter.

She touched his arm. "Hey, I was only kidding."

Her hand lingered, and the way she looked at him with those soft brown eyes made the heat start to rise again.

The knock at the door from room service couldn't have been better timed.

Madison sprang to her feet and headed for the door. With a grin over her shoulder, she said, "By the way, Zang Toi is a man."

6

TWO CUPS OF CAFFEINE may have been a bad idea, Madison realized as she placed her empty cup on the tray room service had left on the glass coffee table. Now she had a real excuse for her hands to shake.

She was still a little rattled from their earlier encounter—she'd never been so unprofessional in her life. All she wanted to do was sit and stare at him, watch his hazel eyes change to that golden color as his passion grew, study the way his lower lip jutted out ever so slightly. She'd never been this sappy with a subject before. Famous or not.

She watched Jack sip his black coffee, the small white china cup looking exceptionally fragile wrapped in his long lean fingers. He got distracted by something outside the window, and the quiet intensity in his eyes made her want to grab her camera.

She moved, and when he paid no attention she did just that. But she got off only one shot before he gave her an annoyed look.

She shrugged. "I couldn't resist."

He didn't seem happy, and she regretted taking advantage of the private moment.

"Okay," she said breezily. "Ready to get back to work?"

"Do I have a choice?"

"I was hoping the coffee would improve your disposition." She bit her lip. Too late. The snide remark was out there weighing down the air between them. What was wrong with her? Why was she behaving like this? Maybe, if she didn't, she'd do something even more foolish...

"I promise it'll improve as soon as this is over." He set down the cup. "Where do you want me?"

"In the bedroom."

His right eyebrow lifted. "Oh, really?"

"Let me get a new roll of film," she murmured when a witty comeback failed her. "I'll meet you in there." She hesitated, and then added, "Feel free to take off your shirt."

The look of astonishment on his face made her feel much better. More in control.

She laughed. "I guess that's a no."

"Depends on whether that's a personal or professional request."

"Which one will get your shirt off?"

He smiled, but before he answered, Madison's cell phone went off, playing Pat Benatar's "Love Is a Battlefield."

She cursed silently for not having turned it off. Really stupid. Nothing was more important than this shoot. She was about to silence it when she noticed it was Karrie calling. In the second that she hesitated, Jack withdrew a cell phone from its case hooked onto his belt, and motioned for her to take the call.

Madison might have resisted, but he'd already started checking his messages. So she quickly answered before voice mail kicked in. "Hey, where have you been?"

"Rob and I were on a dig with some of his students

and I didn't have phone service. I just got your messages. What's going on?"

Madison saw that Jack had wandered toward the bedroom, his phone at his ear, and she continued toward the far corner of the suite for more privacy. "I can't talk long. I'm at a shoot."

"But everything's okay?"

"Oh, yeah."

"Damn, your messages about gave me a heart attack. You sounded…I don't know…frantic."

Madison sighed. "Sorry. I'd just needed to talk to you."

"About what? Wait a minute, is this about Jack Logan? He agreed to the spread?"

"Yep."

"Congratulations." She paused. "Oh, wow, is that the shoot you're on now?"

"Uh-huh."

"Tell me."

"Not a good time." Madison glanced toward the bedroom door. No sign of Jack. A lot of street noise on the line made it difficult to hear. Karrie was obviously traveling. "Are you going to be home tonight?"

"You're not making me wait. Is he as good-looking in person? Ouch." Karrie chuckled. "Rob just pinched my leg."

Madison smiled. As if he had anything to worry about. Karrie was so head-over-heels in love it was almost sickening. Madison had never seen her friend happier. "Tell him I said hey."

"So, tell me about him."

"I can't. Seriously. Look, I'll call you at home later. About five your time?"

"Make it six. We're on our way back to Las Vegas now. Just one more question. Is he the one in the psychic's prediction?"

"Oh, brother."

"Come on, Madison. You can't tell me you don't believe after what happened to me with Rob."

"Coincidence. That's it. Madam Zora got lucky." She glanced over her shoulder, not expecting to find him standing in the middle of the room, staring at her.

He quickly looked away but she wondered how much he'd heard. Not that she'd said anything bad. But still, it was unnerving knowing he'd been the topic of discussion.

"I really have to go now. I'll call you later." She barely heard Karrie say goodbye before Madison severed the connection. "Sorry," she muttered, turned off her phone and stuffed it back in her camera bag.

"I didn't mean to eavesdrop," he said, "but I thought I heard you refer to a Madam Zora."

Just what she needed. To have him think she was some fruitcake who sought advice from psychics. She shrugged. "She was a guest at a party I went to a few months ago. I don't really know her."

"She's the psychic, right?"

"Yeah, I think so." How the hell did he know who she was? The name, of course. After all, how many of her friends were called madam? "Ready to get started?"

His gaze narrowed. He didn't make a move to follow her. "Why were you discussing this woman?"

Madison stared back, dumbfounded by his accusatory tone. "I apologize for taking a call, but that doesn't give you the right to pry into my personal business."

He blinked. "That wasn't my intention."

Then what was up with the questions? She sighed. Better to let it go. More talk would lead back to Madam Z., and she sure didn't want to go there. "Okay, let's just forget it."

"I don't think so."

She stopped and swiveled around to stare at him. He wasn't kidding. The oddest look distorted his face, a little angry, but mostly confused.

"I'd like to know why and with whom you were discussing Madam Zora."

"Why?"

"If you're setting me up, I don't have to tell you our agreement is null."

"I have no idea what you're talking about." She could tell he was serious, and she didn't want to anger him. Which was probably too late, judging by the stern set of his jaw, the suspicion in his eyes. "Really, I don't."

"You say you met this Madam Zora at a party?"

"Yes, a group of women I know take turns giving theme parties. Sonya Zimmerman hired Madam Zora to give readings." She shrugged. "I don't even believe in that nonsense. It was just entertainment."

He seemed to relax, even seemed somewhat interested. "So you had a reading?"

She shrugged. "Only because I had my arm twisted." She vaguely understood his curiosity but she sure didn't want to continue this conversation. "It's almost ten. We really need to get back to work."

"How did she do with the reading? Any accuracy to it? Or did she stick to broad generalities?"

"Why are you so interested?"

He sighed, looking mildly disgusted. "I guess you heard she's the new celebrity fad."

"A friend said something about her being the new psychic to the stars but I figured Shelly had been reading the tabloids again. I mean, the woman had a good gig going. Dressed the part, had the candles and aromatherapy stuff going on, but come on…give me the right props and I could be Madam M."

He smiled. "So you don't believe that some people actually have a gift or sixth sense."

"Of course not." She hesitated, afraid she might have offended him with her disdain. "Do you?"

"No, but I have the dubious pleasure of interviewing the famous Madam Z. next week."

"No way."

He nodded.

"On your show?"

"That's the plan."

"Wow!"

"What?"

Madison shrugged a shoulder, hesitating, wary of offending him. "I didn't figure you for someone who would give a psychic that much credence."

"She's just an assignment. As a matter of fact, I personally think the whole psychic thing is a bunch of bull. The phenomena, however, is fascinating."

"I thought the trend was kind of passé."

His eyebrows lifted in amusement. "How long ago did you have your reading?"

"I told you it wasn't my idea. Plus, I would never have paid for something like that. Now, may we please get to the bedroom?"

"Put that way, how could I resist?"

She heard the humor in his voice but kept walking toward the bedroom without a backward glance. Although she doubted she'd heard the last of his questions regarding Madam Zora.

Madison shuddered at the memory of the psychic's warning. A good-looking man, the animal attraction, being swept away, the inability to reason… That was so not Madison. Of course none of what the woman said had anything to do with Jack Logan, either, for God's sake.

She got to the bedroom and opened the drapes halfway, studied how the light filtered into the room and then made some adjustments. The sun was still low and partially blocked by another building on the next street. Perfect.

They would have to act quickly to capture the way the natural light practically made the bed glow. She turned to find Jack standing at the door watching her.

"I'd like to get a couple of shots with this lighting," she said motioning him over. "But we'll have to really move."

"Where do you want me?"

"Here." She pointed to a corner of the bed where the sunlight hit.

Frowning, he tentatively moved closer. "You want me to sit?"

"Right here."

"And do what?"

"Don't look so worried. Your virtue is safe with me."

He laughed, and damn, she wished she'd had her camera ready. He perched on the corner of the bed as she'd requested, but he still looked tense. Annoyed. As if he'd rather be anywhere but here. Wasn't gonna work.

"Okay," she said, stepping back and readying her camera. "Don't freak out on me, but how about you unbutton your top button?"

"Right."

"Just pretend you're about to get undressed. You don't really have to."

"Gee, thanks."

"Come on." She stayed in focus, waiting. "I'll unbutton mine if you'll unbutton yours."

That startled a laugh out of him and she clicked. "Ah, so this was supposed to be a humorous shot."

"No, but I'll take what I can get." She crouched down to get a different angle and nearly lost her balance.

Jack grabbed her forearm, his strong fingers easily circling the area just above her wrist.

"I'm fine."

He released her, and she fell backward.

Muttering a mild oath, she struggled back up. Well, she had been fine until he touched her.

"Need help?"

The amusement in his voice was enough to give her momentum and she righted herself. "No, thanks."

This wasn't good. Her thoughts kept going back to Madam Zora and her ludicrous prediction and screwing with Madison's concentration. As if her awareness of Jack wasn't already heightened enough. Although it was an interesting challenge to have such a compelling subject.

But this wasn't about her career. The man did funny things to her insides. Made her forget she was a professional. Tempted her with forbidden fruit. Upset her focus. She had to be stronger. Much stronger.

"What exactly are you looking for?" Jack asked after a long silence.

"If I use the 's' word, are you going to get mad?" She didn't need an answer. His reaction was clear in the dip of his brows. "Okay, forget that. Just try to look relaxed. As if you've just returned home after a long day at the office or after walking in Central Park with a friend. You might be absently unbuttoning your shirt to take—"

He shook his head. "Here we go again."

"I'm not asking you to take off your shirt. I mean, I am, but I know you won't, so I just want it to look as if you're unwinding for the day and *about* to change your clothes."

"Why?"

"Because I'm trying to tell a story here." *With pictures.* Just as Madam Z. had pointed out. Oh, no, she couldn't think about that crackpot and her silly prediction again. Not now. She breathed in deeply. "Each picture should show a different side of you."

"I prefer the clothed sides."

"Very funny. Look." She got ahold of his top button before he could say a word and slid it free.

Actually he looked too stunned to stop her. Hadn't even flinched. He only stared at her, his eyes a kaleidoscope of greens and gold and brown, making her knees dangerously weak.

She lowered her hands to her sides. "There. Not so bad, huh?" She took a tentative step back, slowly, testing the strength in her legs before she made a total fool out of herself. "Now if you'll pretend you're about to undo the next button, I'll take a few shots."

He spread his hands. "You want to show me how I should do that, too?"

She couldn't tell if he was angry or teasing her. "I was only trying to break the ice."

"Go ahead. Show me what you want."

"You know…" She fidgeted with the neckline of her T-shirt as if it had buttons.

"Kind of like a striptease?"

Maybe she shouldn't have touched him but now he was ticking her off. "If you want."

JACK COULDN'T HIDE his smile as he watched the storm brewing in her eyes. She was a puzzle for sure. Even though she generally remained professional and composed, he could tell she was uneasy around him.

He wasn't naive about the effect he had on women. Whether he liked it or not. But he didn't think that was the problem with Madison. She was too sure of herself, too goal oriented to let sex or chemistry get in her way.

"I'll pass on that one."

"A pity."

He smiled. "Are you hungry?"

Her eyebrows went up, and her mouth dropped open. "Are you crazy?"

"Well, no, though you're pushing me pretty close to the edge."

She glanced at her watch. "Did you know that it's almost eleven already?"

"Probably why I'm hungry. Your point?"

"I'll be lucky if I have one picture I can use so far."

"You gotta be kidding."

"No, I'm not, but I think you know that."

They glared at each other for a moment. She was right. Jack knew the morning hadn't gone well. He also

knew he was partly to blame. And he realized how ac-
customed he'd become to getting his way. But not this
time. He was locked into this deal. The only saving
grace was Madison. He liked her.

"Okay," he said finally, "for the next half hour we
get as much done as possible. We have lunch at eleven-
thirty."

"I've got a couple of candy bars and some cheese
crackers."

"You actually eat that junk?"

"How hungry are you?"

"Not that hungry." He tapped the face of his watch.
"Better get moving. We have half an hour."

She pressed her lips together, and her breasts rose and
fell with the deep breath she took. His gaze followed the
curve of her neck to the point of her chin where a shal-
low cleft indented her flawless skin. Not particularly noticeable. You had to really look to see it.

Out of nowhere came the sudden urge to lick the
spot. To run his tongue over her lips, to part them and
slip inside. The idea startled him, possessed him, took
such a strong hold of his will it scared the hell out of him.

"Okay," she said in that no-nonsense way of hers.
"It's up to you. Cooperate and you could be wolfing
down a cheeseburger in half an hour."

He wished. "I doubt that."

"Oh, excuse me, I forgot you're a caviar kind of guy."

"No, but my personal trainer is. Actually, he's more
a tuna kind of guy. No mayo. A squirt of lemon juice if
I'm lucky."

"Are you serious?"

"So I exaggerated a little."

She made a face. "That would suck, having someone tell you what you can and can't eat."

"You get used to it."

"If I were making big enough bucks, I might choke down something green and ugh, healthy once in a while."

He laughed and she snapped a shot. Which annoyed him. The moment had felt private, the camera an intrusion.

"No, don't get up." She put a hand on his shoulder. "Let me get a few more shots."

It was only her palm, innocently pressed to his shoulder. Her skin didn't even meet his, but he felt her heat, felt the stirring in his groin.

He rested his hand on the bed, and the silk beneath his fingers made everything worse. It was too easy to picture Madison next to him, the camera forgotten. He'd like to put that impudence of hers to a real test, see how together she'd be with her legs on his shoulders....

"Whoa, that's it," she said. "Give me more. Just like that."

He bit back a groan and prayed her camera wouldn't pick up his humiliation. What was it about this woman that made him so crazy?

7

FIFTEEN MINUTES LATER Madison put down her camera. "I think it's time for lunch."

At her abrupt about-face, Jack narrowed his beautiful hazel eyes, and she had to turn away for fear of doing something totally, irreversibly stupid like giving him a lip-lock that would land them both in the emergency room of New York General.

"Hungry all of a sudden?"

"Yep." She busied herself with carefully stowing her camera, mentally kicking herself for disrupting the flow. She'd gotten some terrific shots. She had no business quitting right now.

He was hot. Five-alarm. Totally stunning. Way past sexy and headed straight for death by orgasm. Any woman with half an X chromosome couldn't look at the pictures Madison had just taken and not ask him to sign her panties.

In the past twenty minutes, something had changed in his attitude and lit his face with a vitality that made flames of desire leap in his eyes, which would burn, no scorch, any unsuspecting woman who gazed too long.

She should forget lunch. Keep shooting until her arms fell off. No, it was better to take a break and lose some momentum than to embarrass herself. Which she was damn close to accomplishing.

"You have something in mind?"

Oh, yeah. She looked up, confirmed it was an innocent question and found she could breathe again. "There's a pizza place around the—ah, I forgot. No pizza."

"No pizza," he repeated with a wry smile. "I've eaten at Amuse Bouche a couple of times. Nice place."

"The restaurant downstairs?"

He nodded.

Oh, God. She hadn't even been brave enough to glance at the menu. An appetizer alone would probably set her back a week's worth of grocery money. That was a lot of candy bars.

"You don't like it there?"

She cleared her throat, while mentally calculating the balance left on her charge card. "Um, no, the food is terrible."

"Really? I thought it was quite—" His frown turned to a smile. "Have you eaten there?"

"Well, no."

"Ah, so maybe your friend Madam Zora predicted you wouldn't like it?"

"Don't go there. I promise it'll get ugly."

Smiling, Jack stood and refastened the top two buttons of his shirt. Such a pity. But it was little details like that that were getting her into trouble. Making her lose her focus. Wasting precious time.

"Come on. Amuse Bouche is close and makes the most sense."

"It's popular." She tried not to sound hopeful. "It may be too crowded."

"It's early yet. I don't think we'll have a problem."

Of course they wouldn't, and it had nothing to do with anything except that he was Jack Logan. She sighed and hoped like hell her credit card could handle lunch.

"MR. LOGAN, NO ONE TOLD ME you'd be joining us." The blond hostess with dark, exotic eyes and pouty lips seemed genuinely contrite as she greeted them with two menus in her hand.

"No problem. Can you feed us?"

"Of course." Her smile included Madison. "Will anyone else be joining you?"

"Just the two of us."

"Would over here be all right?" She gestured toward a table near the center of the room.

Jack frowned briefly and glanced around. Almost every head in the restaurant had turned in their direction. "Do you have anything more private?"

The hostess didn't even blink, just smiled and led them to a table for two toward the back of the restaurant, weaving them between tables and beautifully painted partitions. Madison loved the gorgeous black urns with the dried flower arrangements, pink, of course.

The hostess gave him a dazzling smile. "Is this satisfactory?"

"Perfect." Jack pulled out Madison's chair, which she really hated because it always seemed awkward to have someone hold your chair while you tried to get into a comfortable position.

But she smiled, thanked him and waited until he went to take his own seat before she scooted her chair closer to the table.

The hostess handed them each a menu, and Madison's gaze locked on the right side. The prices shocked her, which was pretty bad considering she'd lived in New York her whole life.

"I'm sure there's something on the menu you'll find bearable," Jack said, watching her, an amused glint in his eyes.

Yeah, like water. From the tap. It had to be free. The waiter or waitress would look down their nose at her, but she could take it. Better than her pocketbook could take a hefty bill. "I don't trust a place that doesn't have malted milk on the menu."

He smiled. "Their Bananas Foster may cure you of that notion."

"I doubt it," she muttered, scanning the menu for the desserts. Which, of course, weren't there. Places like this had a separate dessert menu. Probably just so they could charge double. "Does your personal trainer know about your penchant for the Bananas Foster?"

"Funny." His gaze flickered to the left before he abruptly returned his attention to the menu, and she got the feeling he was more interested in escaping the curious glances than in the selections.

She hoped, anyway. Kit, Hush's PR person had set this up. Madison should have talked to her about running a tab for the day that Madison could take care of later in private. Maybe it wasn't too late. Maybe they could even bill her. She expected a check from Shelly in three days. She felt stupid for not having anticipated a situation like this. Guys like Jack Logan didn't grab a slice of pizza at the corner greasy spoon.

"How hungry are you?" he asked absently.

"Why?"

"I thought we'd split an appetizer. How do the crab cakes sound?"

Expensive. "Would you excuse me for a moment? I have a little business to take care of."

He looked up in surprise. "Now?"

"I'll only be a minute. I'll be back by the time you order the crab cakes."

"Don't leave me."

That stopped her and she sank back into her seat. The nosy couple at the next table apparently heard and, grinning, whispered something to each other.

Jack flashed her a sheepish smile. "You leave and it'll be open season."

She knew what he meant. The way some women acted around him made Madison ashamed of her gender. They may have been dressed in designer clothes but they were really no better than the guys working along Columbus Circle who irritated her with their loud and obnoxious remarks.

"I'll only be gone for a couple of minutes. Promise."

"Don't make me beg," he said, his voice lowered, his eyes twinkling with humor.

"I'd like to see that."

He leaned back. "You would, wouldn't you?"

"I was kidding." She scoffed, offended that he looked serious, and then the corners of his mouth curved. She got up again, leaned over and whispered. "I'm leaving you to the wolves."

"Come on." He touched her arm, persuasively stroking his thumb over her wrist. "I'm sure whatever you have to do can wait."

"Are you?" she asked archly, impressed that she was able to maintain her cool when she really wanted to melt right there. In the restaurant. In front of everyone. And all he was doing was touching her wrist.

"If that sounded arrogant, it's only because I'm desperate." He gave her one of those million-dollar grins.

"Did you know that half the people in the restaurant are staring at us?"

He blinked and released her. "Great."

"No one's got a camera, though. So it'll all be hearsay when it hits the papers."

"Don't be so sure. There's paparazzi under every rock."

"So tell them I'm your sister, or personal assistant."

"Yeah, right." The way he ran his gaze down the front of her shirt made her nipples tighten.

She took a deep steadying breath. "All right then. I'll be back in two minutes."

"You won't, but go ahead."

"Wanna bet?"

"Sure."

"That was rhetorical."

"I'll bet you lunch."

"Lunch?" Her heart lifted. She shouldn't, really.

He nodded. "If you're back in under two minutes, I buy. If you're not, you buy."

This was too easy. The hell with pride. She glanced at her watch. "You're on."

He smiled, checked his Rolex, and said, "On your mark…"

She grabbed her camera bag, wove her way through the restaurant and headed straight for the ladies' room. No need to track down Kit now. Madison had every in-

tention of making it back to the table with lots of time
to spare.

She studied her reflection in the mirror and saw that
she could use a touch of blush and maybe some gloss.
She needed mascara and liner, too, but she didn't have
time for an entire makeover. Too obvious, anyway. She
checked her watch before she got busy with a couple of
subtle touch-ups to brighten her face. Then she bent at
the waist and fluffed out her hair.

Only briefly did she suffer a pang of guilt. It probably
was unprofessional to let him pay for lunch. On the other
hand, if he hadn't been so difficult she would've gotten
all the shots she needed already and lunch wouldn't be an
issue. Okay, so that was weak, but she was sticking to it.

By the time she returned, people had started to line
up near the door, hoping for a table. She slipped by
them and suffered another pang of guilt when she saw
that a blonde had claimed Madison's seat across from
Jack, who, to his credit, maintained a poker face and
didn't look as if he wanted to reach across the table and
strangle the woman. Of course, on a scale of one to ten,
the blonde was probably a twelve.

Madison got closer and tried not to stare at the
woman's breasts. They couldn't be real. Not a chance.
Anything that huge would be headed for her waist instead of pointing perkily at Jack.

He caught Madison's eye, and relief boyishly flooded
his face, but only for an instant, and then he was Jack
Logan again, television's morning heartthrob. Calm,
cool, collected.

The tiny private look into the man made her heart
flutter. It was hardly invitational. Yet she'd seen enough

to know he allowed very little emotion to escape. Liked to keep the public at a distance. But he'd allowed her that one small peek.

And she'd be a total fool to read anything into it.

"Check your watch," she said. "I don't want you welching on our bet."

The blonde looked up but didn't make a move to leave.

"Hi, I'm Madison Tate." She offered her hand, which was received with a surprisingly firm grip.

"Moira Atkins." She stayed put for several moments, but then when Jack started to get up, she finally got a clue and stood. "Sorry, didn't mean to interrupt." She smiled at Jack. "Call me."

"I see what you mean," Madison murmured as she reclaimed her chair and watched Moira's curvy backside sway across the restaurant. "These women move fast."

He picked up a business card lying on the table beside a glass of orange juice and slipped it into his breast pocket. "She's an agent."

"I thought Larry was your agent."

"He is."

"You're not going to dump him."

He narrowed his gaze. "Why would you care?"

"I liked him. That's all." Shrugging, she picked up the menu. "Did you order anything yet?"

"I'm not dumping Larry. I get solicited by the new up-and-comers all the time."

"Pretty nervy of them, isn't it? I mean, I'd think having an agent is sort of like having a partner. You just don't jump from one—" She stopped herself short. Obviously none of this was any of her business. "Have you ordered anything besides juice?"

"I totally agree. Larry and I look out for each other."

"Yeah, I know. When I first queried him about the shoot, he had so many questions you'd think I was asking for his permission to marry you."

Jack smiled. "We've been together a long time."

"Longer than most married couples according to him."

"I've heard that a few times. He's a good guy and a good friend. I trust him. We're in it together for the long haul."

Madison smiled at the affection in his voice. She liked his attitude toward friendship. That said a lot about him.

"Are you ready to order?"

They both looked up at the waitress, Jack appearing as startled as Madison at the woman's presence.

Her nametag said Tara, and just like the rest of the hotel's employees she was gorgeous. "I can come back in a few minutes."

Jack nodded. "Thank you."

Madison concentrated on the menu. Not that much of it appealed to her. She'd have been happier with an order of fries than a plate of crab-stuffed mushrooms. She didn't even bother to check out the salads. Yuck. Of course a cup of blue cheese dressing just about made any salad bearable.

"Would you like me to make a couple of suggestions?" he asked, and she looked up to see if he was making fun of her. "You look indecisive."

"Nope. I know what I want." She set the menu aside. "And you?"

"Ready."

"Okay." She saw that Tara had stopped at another table. "Let's talk about this afternoon. I'm thinking the spa should be next."

"Fine." He leaned forward, and lowered his voice. "Now tell me about Madam Zora."

Madison groaned. "I thought we'd settled that. I don't know the woman. I only met her briefly."

"But she gave you a reading."

"It was nonsense."

"Tell me about it."

"I don't remember."

He smiled. "Yes, you do."

"Excuse me?"

"You might not have liked what she said, but you remember."

"Says who?"

"I heard you on the phone."

"Nice." She tried to recall what she'd said to Karrie. Nothing incriminating. At least not when he was in the room. Where the hell was that waitress?

"Don't forget that I interview people for a living." Jack caught her eye and held on to her gaze. He looked pretty serious. "I'm damn good at it, too."

"Why on earth would it matter what that woman said to me?"

"I want to get a feel for her style. How broad she keeps her predictions, how accurate she is about personal information." He sighed and glanced around. "To tell you the truth, I don't want to come off like a total skeptic when I interview her."

The waitress showed up, and Jack immediat[ely] leaned back and fell silent. While she took their or[der] Madison tried to decide what to tell him. He seem[ed] nest enough. She could tell him about Karrie.

As soon as Tara disappeared, Jack was b[ack] on his

game. He leaned forward, determination in his eyes. "You said something to your friend about Madam Zora getting lucky. May I assume there was some accuracy to her prediction?"

"Yes, but it could easily have been coincidence."

"That said..." He gestured impatiently for her to continue.

"Okay, so my friend Karrie is attractive, late twenties, obviously single since she was my date for the party," she said, and ignored his attempt to hold back a smile. "So how far a stretch was it for Madam Z. to predict she would meet some hunky guy, fall in love and live happily ever after?"

"From what the women in the office say, around here that's a rarity."

Madison stifled a laugh. "You've got me there. But Karrie didn't meet Rob here in Manhattan. She knew him from college back in Las Vegas."

"So didn't Madam Zora know he would be a man from your friend's past?" he asked, the question clearly rhetorical, judging by the smug expression on his face.

"Actually, she did."

His gaze narrowed. He leaned closer. "What exactly did she tell your friend?"

Madison shrugged. "That she'd return to the desert and would hook up with this guy she knew. Turned out he was her former archaeology professor." Goose bumps rose on Madison's arms when she remembered nother small detail. She laughed nervously. If she told r, it would sound crazy. He'd probably think she was *this* bng with him. Or worse, that she really believed in ney.

"What? You remembered something."

"You won't believe me."

He frowned with impatience. "What is it?"

"She knew Rob's initials," she said slowly, and when his frown deepened, she added, "Madam Zora told Karrie the man she'd meet again would have the initials R.P. But of course Karrie didn't make the connection that night at the party. She hadn't seen or thought of Rob for over eight years."

His brows dipped as he digested the information. "So how did they meet up again?"

"Karrie was sent to Las Vegas on business. In fact, her company sent her to specifically meet with Rob concerning a piece of land where he wanted to conduct a dig with his students."

"How long after Madam Zora's prediction did that happen?"

Madison shrugged. "About three months maybe."

"Interesting." He thought for a moment. "Anyway Madam Zora could have known that Karrie's company would be sending her to—"

Madison shook her head. "No way. She didn't know. Her boss didn't know. Karrie had always sworn she'd never go back west. Everything just sort of happened."

"Do you have a pen and piece of paper?"

"I think so." She lifted the camera bag strap off the back of her chair and quickly found a pen and an old to-do list. "This is all I have," she said, handing it to him. "The back of the paper is clean."

He started scribbling right away and she leane ward for a peek. Except it looked like some sort sonal shorthand and she couldn't make it out.

"Let's go over this again," he said. "Just the highlights."

"Yes, sir."

He looked up, surprised, and then he smiled. "Please."

She smiled back. "But I've already told you everything."

"Humor me."

She sighed, staring into his beautiful eyes, knowing she was the envy of every woman in the room, and he wanted to talk about psychics. Okay, so that was pretty much the way her life went. Nothing new.

"Karrie and I went to this party. She made me go with her to have a reading. Madam Zora told her she would be having this torrid affair with someone from her past."

"You didn't tell me about the torrid affair part."

"Is it important?"

He chuckled. "I guess not."

"Do you want me to continue or not?"

"I won't interrupt again." He pressed his lips together, looking so boyishly adorable she wanted to lean across the table and kiss him.

Of course she wanted to do that, anyway. She sighed, forced her attention back to their conversation. "Okay, let's see— Oh, yeah, I have to give Madam Z. her props here. She knew that Karrie's brother was a pilot. No one else at the party would have known that." She shrugged at the astonishment on his face. "Although, the way she put it was that he was content to soar like a bird, or something like that."

"That's pretty remarkable."

"But she didn't specifically say he was a pilot either."

He studied her with far too much interest.

"You realize you interrupted again," she said, and he

smiled. "Then you know the rest. Karrie was supposed to hook up with someone from her past with the initials R.P., they'd have an affair and yada, yada, yada."

"So basically everything Madam Zora predicted would happen did, in fact, happen."

"Well, yeah. Sort of." Why in the hell had she allowed this conversation to continue? She looked around for the waitress. Madison needed dessert. She'd heard the Death by Chocolate was to die for. Why not? He was buying.

"And you still don't believe that this woman has some kind of sixth sense?"

"She got lucky. That's all."

He blinked, confusion flickering in his face. "You don't want to believe." He narrowed his gaze and stared at her with fascination. "What did this woman predict for you?"

Heat crawled up her neck and into her face. She was probably as red as a cherry tomato, which in itself told him more than she wanted him to know, but she'd die a thousand deaths before she admitted what Madam Z. had said.

"Tell me, Madison," he whispered. "Did it have anything to do with me?"

8

JACK WATCHED THE TIPS of her ears redden. He'd never seen anyone blush so completely like that before. She'd obviously had a whopper of a reading that still resonated. A gentleman would back off. He couldn't help himself. "What did she tell you?"

"None of your business."

"So you do believe there might be something to her prediction."

"No."

"Then why not tell me?"

"Okay, she said I was gonna be president of the United States."

He laughed. "Which year?"

"She wasn't specific. Told you she's a fraud."

"Madison, you have to tell me."

"See? That's where you're wrong. I don't. Where's Tara? I'm starving."

"You're stalling, trying to come up with a phony story," he accused, studying her closely. To her credit she stayed with him. Didn't try to break eye contact. "That, of course, I won't buy for a second."

Her chin lifted a fraction. "She said my career was on an upswing, that I'd be fabulously successful one day and I'd also have a wildly intense affair with a co-worker. I freelance. That obviously won't happen."

There was more to it. No matter how blank she schooled her expression, the lingering pink in her cheeks gave her away. "I'm sure you pointed that out to her."

"I didn't waste my time."

"If that's it, why were you so reluctant to tell me?"

She blinked and looked away. "I don't know."

"Look, I'm not trying to make you uncomfortable. I'm just making a point. As much of a skeptic as you claim to be, she clearly did get to you."

She made a face. "Okay, after what happened to Karrie, yeah, I did think twice. But I know better."

He smiled. "Okay."

"Now can we strategize our afternoon, or did you want to have to spend all night here?"

The thought appealed more than it should. Even his body reacted to the idea of spending the night with her. Up in the Haiku Suite. Naked. Tangled together in the satin sheets.

He mentally shook himself. She hadn't given any signals that she was interested. She'd maintained a professional distance. What the hell was wrong with him? He knew lots of guys who traded on their celebrity and screwed any woman they could. He wasn't one of them.

In fact, celebrity tended to put a crimp in his love life. He seldom dated. Too many nasty repercussions if the relationship failed. He'd already had one horrific experience, the details of which had ended up splashed across the tabloids. Half of it was even true, thanks to Alyssa, the woman he'd thought he could trust. The woman with whom he'd once imagined spending the rest of his life.

Her ultimate greed, manipulation and deceit disabused him of the notion. He'd heard she'd received a hundred grand for the article. His only consolation was that amount wasn't nearly enough to accommodate her lifestyle. She'd probably gone through the entire sum in a month.

"Look, the idea doesn't appeal to me, either, okay? So let's decide how we want to best use our time."

He looked blankly at Madison and realized how deeply he'd sunk into his own thoughts. It took him a moment to get it together. "You mean I start getting a say?"

"You're kidding, right?" She scoffed. "Honey, if I were running the show, you would've had your shirt off already."

The couple at the next table both shot startled glances at them.

Jack sighed. "I don't think you said that loudly enough."

Madison bit her lower lip. "I have this sudden urge to babble an explanation that I'm a photographer and we're doing a shoot upstairs."

"No."

"Of course not."

"Let it go."

"Right." She groaned softly. "Sorry."

Any other time, hell, with any other woman, he'd have been furious. The tabloid vultures made up enough lies without being fed overheard conversations. But he couldn't be angry with Madison. Not when she looked so miserable. "Hey, cheer up. There is a Santa Claus."

"I know. He was my date last New Year's Eve." Her lips started to curve. "I'm not saying another word until we get upstairs."

"I feel another bet coming on."

"Don't try and get out of lunch. You're still buying."

Before he could say anything, their food came, and Madison didn't hesitate to dig with gusto into her seafood crepes. Extra sauce, extra cheese, extra butter for her rolls, she wanted it all. He was both fascinated and amazed at her lack of inhibition. She wasn't sloppy or anything. She simply ate like a normal person. Not like so many other women he ate lunch or dinner with, who picked at their food and ate like they didn't want to mess up their lipstick.

She'd be like that in bed. Uninhibited. Taking what she wanted. Asking for more. Giving it her all.

Heat pooled in his gut, shot to his groin.

He lowered his gaze to concentrate on his Chilean sea bass and tried not to look at her glistening lower lip. Shoved the dangerous thoughts from his mind. He had to keep this professional. Maybe later they could have dinner sometime, go to the theater or take a picnic lunch to Central Park.

Get naked.

Christ. This had to stop.

"IF YOU WANT DESSERT, speak up now because I'm asking for the check."

Madison blinked, looking slightly taken aback. And rightfully so. He'd unintentionally come off abrupt.

"I'm good for now," she said. "I've got a couple of candy bars in my bag."

He shook his head and watched her furtively try to sop up the remaining sauce with a piece of her roll. Mission accomplished, she plopped it into her mouth and then touched the pink linen napkin to her lips. She caught him watching and smiled.

"I'd like to see some of your work sometime," he said before he knew he was going to say it.

"My work?"

"Your portfolio."

"Uh, well, I normally shoot by assignment." She shrugged. "Or sometimes I get lucky and sell an unsolicited photograph."

"Which means you probably have a whole collection of great shots."

"I wouldn't call them great. Do you really want to see them?"

"Yes, I do."

"Why?"

He wasn't sure how to answer. Because he wanted some insight into the woman? Maybe because he wanted a reason to see her again? "I don't know," he said truthfully.

"Oh. Well, okay then. Sure."

"I've made you uncomfortable."

"No, I just—no one's ever asked to see my pictures before."

"Probably because you have them plastered all over the walls of your apartment so no one has to."

She laughed. "Yeah, right."

"No?"

"A big no." Her gaze shifted away as if she wanted to drop the subject.

The check arrived, and after he'd settled up, he obliged Madison by keeping the conversation directed to the shoot as they left the table and headed for the elevators.

They didn't get far when a pair of stunning young women intercepted them. Both tall and blond, they looked as if they could be sisters.

"Mr. Logan," the slightly shorter one said, "would it be too much trouble to get an autograph from you?"

He hated this part of the job. He really did. But he smiled and accepted the small sheet of cream-colored linen stationery she handed him. "No problem."

"Me, too, if you don't mind," the other one said, already having withdrawn a similar piece of stationery only this one a lime green.

"Okay," he said, not liking the way they'd seemed to edge Madison out of the picture. She didn't look offended though, but simply stood to the side watching with undisguised interest.

"Sorry," he said pointedly. "I'll only be a minute."

"Take your time."

The other two turned and looked at her, and she smiled at them and then glanced at her watch. She seemed indifferent to their quick dismissal and dug in her bag producing her cell phone.

"Christina, that's my name," one of the women said. "And could you add—"

"Sorry, no special requests." He flashed her a smile to soften the words. "I don't want to keep the lady waiting." He scribbled his name for each of them and handed the autographs back to the unpleasantly surprised pair.

Too bad. Normally he was more accommodating but he didn't like the way they'd treated Madison, as if she were unimportant. A nobody. It didn't matter that she didn't seem to care. He did.

"You didn't have to rush," she said, glancing over her

shoulder at the other two as he took her elbow and urged her toward the elevators.

"They got what they wanted."

She laughed. "I don't think so."

He shook his head and tamped down a smile.

"What do these women do, keep a supply of stationery on them and stalk celebs?"

He depressed the elevator button. "I noticed that. Usually I get a napkin or the back of a receipt."

"Which reminds me, I have a friend named Shelly who'd love an autograph from you."

"And you? Don't you want my autograph?"

Her lips parted. Nothing came out. And then, "Um, well—"

He chuckled. "I'm kidding."

She elbowed him in the ribs as they stepped into the elevator, and he grunted. She rolled her eyes and punched the button to the fifteenth floor. "That could've been a lot harder but I didn't wanna damage the merchandise."

With mock hurt he reared his head back. "Is that all I am to you?"

"The truth?"

He frowned. "Maybe not in this case."

"Chicken." She had a great smile. Even when she tried not to and the corners of her mouth quivered slightly, almost grudgingly, as if she wanted everyone to think she was tougher than she was.

She turned her head, and their noses nearly met. Whatever she'd been about to say died on her lips. Her lashes fluttered and she abruptly looked straight ahead.

He let the awkward moment pass, disconcerted by his own reaction. If she'd given even the slightest encouragement, he would have kissed her. Which would pretty much screw up the rest of the day. Of course, his growing fascination with her alone was enough to upset the balance.

What was wrong with him? It wasn't as if he was the kind of guy who couldn't have a platonic relationship with a woman. He'd had many over the years. His secretary, to whom he was like an older brother, was a great example.

Since Lana had started working for him nine months ago, he'd had dinner three or four times with her and her husband and twins. By the second time, the boys had started calling him Uncle Jack.

The elevator stopped four floors later and he absently started to get off. Madison laid a hand on his arm, but two laughing couples carrying glasses of wine rushed into the cab effectively cutting him off.

Startled at their presence, the short brunette splashed half her chardonnay across the front of Jack's shirt. He automatically moved back. Right into Madison. Pinning her against the wall of the cab. Her hands came up and spanned his upper back.

"I am so sorry." The twenty-something brunette clasped a hand over her mouth.

"Come on, Vicki, watch where you're going." A short stocky guy wearing a shirt that was too tight shook his head. "Sorry about my wife. I think she's had one too many."

"Oh, and you haven't." His wife smacked his arm sending another wave of chardonnay over the rim of her glass.

Everyone jerked away, including Jack. Behind him he heard Madison moan softly.

He could barely glance over his shoulder. "Sorry."

"It's okay. You didn't do anything," she whispered, her warm breath dancing across the skin behind his neck and tickling his ear.

His groin tightened and he exhaled slowly.

She'd lowered her hands and he could feel her breasts pressed against his back. Tempted to turn around and feel her softness against his chest, he gritted his teeth and thought about getting out of the elevator and waiting for another one.

"Vicki, you crazy klutz, you're making a mess," the guy said, half laughing, his words slightly slurred. "Looks like I'm gonna have to use the whip and handcuffs on you yet."

"Stop it." Vicki laughed and sent Jack and Madison a sheepish look.

"What? It's no secret. They have the same things in their room." He drained his wine.

Jack cringed. This was exactly the kind of association he didn't want. Fortunately, it didn't seem as if they'd recognized him. He looked down, checked his watch and pretended to fiddle with it to avoid eye contact.

"No, Tom, I think she meant she'd rather you use the feathers instead of the whip," the woman with black curly hair said just as the elevator stopped on the seventh floor.

The guy she was with cursed. "Which one of you morons pressed the wrong floor?"

"Excuse me but there are other people in here." Vicki smiled at Jack and crowded to the side. "You want out?"

He was about to take his opportunity to escape when Madison leaned out and said, "We're going to the fifteenth."

"Ah, to the high-rent digs. Must be nice." The dark-haired woman narrowed her gaze on Jack. "Oh, my God, you're—" She had the gall to move obnoxiously closer. "I know you. Aren't you...?"

Madison squeezed out from behind him. "Yeah, that's him," she said, and before he could strangle her, she let out this annoying and unnatural girlish laugh. "Really," Madison added eagerly.

Skepticism immediately creased the woman's face, and Jack realized what Madison was doing.

Vicki peered closer just as the elevator doors closed and it was too late to escape. "Yeah, you do kind of look like him."

"Who?" both guys asked at once.

Vicki eyed Madison before returning her probing blue gaze to Jack. "You probably get mistaken for him a lot, huh?"

Jack shrugged, trying to look bored. "Especially here in the city."

"Who the hell are you talking about?" the guy she was with demanded, his wine-laden breath foul in the small space.

"Jack Logan!" Glancing at Jack, Vicki bit her lip but couldn't keep from smiling.

The guy frowned while sizing up Jack. "That news-man? Hell, even I could tell that's not him. Logan's shorter and heavier."

Jack just smiled. This wasn't all bad. Not with Madison snuggled up against him. He moved to the side so that he could slip an arm around her. Her eyes widened slightly and then she played the game by smiling back. Even flattened her palm across his belly.

Mostly due to the lack of room, he knew, but he liked the contact. Liked that they could play the role without consequence.

The elevator stopped again and the dark-haired woman and her companion got out, neither of them walking particularly steady.

"We'll see you guys at the pool in ten minutes," Vicki called after them.

The woman grabbed the guy's backside and laughed when he nearly fell into a plant. "Make it an hour."

"Twenty minutes should do it," he said over his shoulder, and the woman smacked his arm.

The elevator doors closed, and Vicki sighed. "Remember when we used to be like that?"

Tom snorted. "What?"

"Like before we were married."

They continued to go back and forth, but Jack wasn't listening. Not when Madison stood so close that he could smell the chocolate mint that had come with the check on her breath. Not when he could feel her heat so close to his crotch that he had to struggle for control.

He looked at her at the same time she looked up at him and without hesitation he brushed his lips across hers. She blinked and stiffened. Let her think it was for show. Let her think whatever the hell she wanted. He had to concentrate on not going back for more.

The elevator dinged, and right before the doors opened, Vicki gave him a final inquisitive look. "Are you sure you aren't…?"

"Come on." Her husband grabbed her around the waist and hauled her out of the car. "It's not him," he said as they headed down the corridor. A second before the doors closed again, he added, "A guy like Logan wouldn't be with a woman like that."

Jack felt as if the air had been knocked out of him. He wanted to punch the guy in his big mouth. Coward that he was, he wanted to disappear suddenly and not have to look into Madison's hurt face.

She pulled away from him and unnecessarily punched the already lit button to their floor. Painful as it was, he forced himself to look at her.

She smiled. "They're tipsy enough, they didn't recognize you."

He nodded, not sure what to say. Maybe she hadn't heard the rude remark.

"Well, at least we know to stay away from the pool for a while."

"Yeah." He let silence fill the air between them, and stared up at the lights signaling the passing of each floor.

"Jack?"

"Yeah."

"Don't worry about it, okay?"

He gazed into her eyes and saw quiet acceptance. She'd heard the buffoon, all right, but she was too gracious to let the thoughtless remark take purchase. "Like you said, they're tipsy. Besides, that guy's an idiot."

She laughed softly. "My hero."

The teasing in her face helped him relax. But he still wouldn't mind planting his fist in the guy's nose. He really was an idiot. How could he say that about Madison? Anyone with half a brain could see the intelligence and humor in her face, the brilliance of her smile. Jack hardly knew her and he could see it as plain as day.

"Hey. Pay attention." She grinned. "We're here."

The doors had opened.

Oh, he was paying attention all right. Maybe too much.

9

MADISON USED THE KEY CARD to open the suite door and told herself for the tenth time that she absolutely would not allow that bigmouthed blowhard to ruin her day. After all, he hadn't said anything she didn't already know. And besides, she accepted her limitations. Fortunately, looks weren't that important to her.

She went in ahead of Jack and as she turned back toward him, she got a whiff of the wine soaking the left front of his shirt. "Whoa! Good thing you brought an extra shirt. You're gonna have to get that one off."

One eyebrow went up and then he glanced down at his shirt. He sniffed and frowned. "I see what you mean."

"To think we actually drink that stuff."

"Somehow it smells different in a glass."

"Amen."

He closed the door behind him. "I'll change, then."

"Right." She didn't know why it suddenly seemed awkward but it did. Maybe he thought she'd gone overboard in playing her role. It had been kind of nice being able to snuggle up to him. To feel the pressure of his backside against her thighs. The mere memory got her heated and she hurried away from him. "I'll get my camera out of the bedroom and reload it in here while you change."

He didn't respond but when she got into the room, she realized he'd followed her. She grabbed her camera and turned to go and saw that he was already pulling off his shirt.

She swallowed. Tried not to stare as more and more muscled belly was revealed. And pecs. Perfect pecs. Sinfully perfect. God bless his personal trainer. She sucked in her stomach and swore she'd give up candy bars. As soon as she polished off the supply in her bag.

Jack yanked his shirt off the rest of the way and rolled it up. Their eyes met and he smiled. She nearly didn't trust her legs to move. In fact, she didn't seem to be going anywhere.

She moistened her suddenly parched lips. "My compliments to your trainer."

He frowned blankly and then chuckled. "I'll let him know you approve. Although he doesn't work nearly as hard as I do."

She couldn't help giving him another once-over. "Why the hell wouldn't you want me to take a few shots without your shirt?"

His smile vanished and he reached for the small bag he'd brought.

She sighed. "That was really stupid."

"Yes, it was."

"Please don't put your shirt on yet. Shouldn't I get points for humility and honesty?"

"You're not taking any shots of me without my shirt."

"Oh, I know. I just wanted to stare for a while. You're so pretty."

Laughing, he shook his head while he withdrew the fresh shirt. Obviously, he thought she was teasing. Good thing. Once again she'd opened her mouth before thinking. That wasn't the worst of it. The nearly uncontrollable urge to run her palms over the ridges in his belly shook her all the way down to her toes.

As soon as he pulled the shirt over his head and drew it down, she went into mourning. He truly was beautiful. One shot of that incredible, mouth-watering chest would be enough to get her the cover. Assuming her pounding heart survived long enough to develop the film.

"All right. Where do you want me?"

Oh, boy, he so didn't want to hear her answer. She turned away so he couldn't see her smile. "Actually, I'd initially thought about moving to the spa but we'd better stay here where it's safer."

A wry smile curved his mouth. "There is no safe place."

"You're right. Take your shirt off again and I'm jumping your bones."

"Promise?"

At the roguish glint in his eyes her heart somersaulted. Ignoring him, she went to the window and opened the drapes halfway. "Over here. We'll take a shot of you looking out of the window."

She turned to find his belt unbuckled and him unzipping his pants. She could only stare, her stomach twisting and knotting so she couldn't speak or move.

And then he tucked in his shirt and pulled up the zipper.

A strangled laugh escaped her. "Be right back."

"Madison?"

"Just a minute." Thankfully she made it to the parlor without hyperventilating or doing anything incredibly embarrassing.

She took a couple of deep breaths, then took a couple more before grabbing one of their used coffee cups and a saucer off the room service tray. The cup had residue from a drip down the side, which she took care of with the linen napkin before returning to the room.

"Here," she said, approaching him, her composure restored. "Pretend you're sipping from the cup as you look out the window."

"We did a 'looking out the window' shot already."

"We're doing another one."

"I see that." Sighing, he took the cup but not the saucer. "Are we almost done?"

"What do you think?"

He gave her an impatient look, and then walked over to the window and stood stiff as a statute.

"Very funny." She set the saucer aside and got her camera. "If you want to ever get out of here, cooperation is the name of the game."

"Hey, I've been pretty good."

"Right. Turn toward the window."

He obliged, but not before giving her a long, measuring look that set her insides tingling.

"Okay, now raise the cup halfway to your lips." She focused. "Could you not look as if you hate the city...the world...life in general?"

"Why?"

She had to laugh. He did, too, and she got a fantastic shot. "Okay, stay with me." She snapped another, and then another.

Even though he was looking at her and not out the window, the sudden kaleidoscope of emotion in his face was exactly what she was looking for. But after several more shots, his face tightened. The magic was gone.

She slowly lowered the camera. What had just happened? Their eyes met briefly and then he looked away—he was the moodiest man she'd ever met.

She understood that some people simply couldn't relax in front of the camera. Obviously he wasn't one of them. He made his living doing live TV, for goodness' sake.

"Why are you so tense all of a sudden?" she asked, a bit too snappishly. So she added, "Tell me what I can do to make you relax."

He blinked, his keen eyes gleaming, and then his mouth curved in a sexy smile that had her gulping hard. "I can think of several things."

"Such as?"

One eyebrow went up. "You don't do coy well."

She gaped in disbelief. "You're not suggesting—" She couldn't finish her thought. It was too absurd. Her heart flip-flopped.

"Actually, I am."

Madison didn't know what to say. She just stared, waiting for him to start laughing or something. But he didn't. In fact, he seemed shockingly serious.

"Okay, enough joking around." Frustrated and more than a little flustered, she took the coffee cup from him. If he wanted to play games, she knew just how to shut him up. "Here, let's try this."

His startled expression was almost satisfaction enough. "What's that?"

"Stay where you are but I want you to put your left hand in your pocket."

He frowned, but did as she asked.

"Now use your other hand to kind of comb your hair back." When he didn't move, she tilted her head to the side and pushed her fingers through her own hair and said, "Like this."

"No way."

"What?"

"I'm not posing like that."

"Cliché, I know, but—"

"It's ridiculous."

She sighed and lowered her hand. Odd, she knew she'd get this reaction, that he'd balk at the sexy pose, but now she really wanted that particular picture. "How many variations have you seen of that pose in different magazines? Because it works. It's time honored. It's not ridiculous." She groaned at the stubbornness on his face. "We don't necessarily have to use the shot but I really want this. Please, Logan."

He stared at her for what seemed an eternity and then quietly said, "Okay."

She grinned. "Okay."

He stretched out his neck, rolled his shoulders, inhaled deeply, as if he were preparing to get into a boxing ring instead of striking a simple pose. His left hand was still jammed in his pocket balled so tightly she could see a fist, and he used his right hand to woodenly cup the back of his head.

She tried not to laugh. But she couldn't help it and a strangled giggle escaped her.

He quickly lowered his hand and withdrew the other from his pocket, muttering, "I told you this was ridiculous."

"No, you're making it ridiculous." She tried not to

even smile or she'd end up giggling more. "Relax, would you?"

"You're right. I am tense." He stretched this way and that and grimaced. "It would help if you rubbed my shoulders."

She rolled her eyes.

"I'm serious. I'm all knotted up. It's a chronic problem I have."

Against her better judgment, she set aside her camera. She gingerly cupped her hands on his shoulders and slid her palms toward his neck. His muscles were tight all right, but not just from tension. Hard and defined, they made her gliding palms itch to connect with bare skin.

"You'll have to do better than that. I won't break."

"Um, I think you're gonna have to sit down. It's hard to get a good grip at this angle."

He didn't hesitate, but instead of taking the chair, he sat on the corner of the bed.

No big deal, really. Except that she had the sudden urge to push him back and tear off his clothes. Of course, that would probably put an end to the shoot, and she really needed to pay her rent for the next few months.

He spread his legs and dropped his chin to his chest. "Right here is the worst of it," he said, indicating the area where his neck and shoulder joined. "Don't be afraid to really dig in. I like a hard massage."

"Yes, sir."

"Look, I wouldn't ask you to do this except we're obviously not going to get anywhere unless I loosen up."

"With all the working out you do I'm surprised you're not more relaxed."

"Believe me, it would be a lot worse if I didn't work out or have a masseuse pound on me twice a week."

"Job pressure?"

He hesitated. "Maybe."

Apparently she was getting too personal. Still, she wondered what had him wound so tight. Of course being in his position probably was enough to keep a person on edge. "Just remember this is cutting into shooting time, and—" She stabbed a particularly stubborn knot with her thumb and he groaned.

"Sorry."

"No, go for it. The harder the better."

Her mind shot off in a totally different direction and she bit her lip. Man, did she have to get a grip on herself. She couldn't get off track, not with so little time.... Maybe he was trying to distract her. Maybe she should call his bluff. They could screw like bunnies for an hour, get it out of their systems and then finish the shoot. Would make for some interesting pictures.

He hunched forward. "That spot right between the shoulder blades...yeah, that's it."

She used as much pressure as she could while standing at such an odd angle. He moaned softly, almost erotically, and she counted to ten in Spanish, then in French, then German and finally in Japanese. That's all the languages she knew up to ten, although she could probably get to twenty in Spanish. But it wasn't going to help.

Even while she distracted herself, her body had a memory of its own. Her nipples had tightened and her mouth had gone completely dry. Each time she rubbed his back harder, she seemed to unconsciously lean closer, her breasts coming dangerously close to grazing his back.

Briefly she wondered how he'd react. She could test the waters by pressing against him and pretend it was an accident. But she'd only end up hurting herself. The day had been murderous enough already without incurring more awkward moments or tension.

"Hmm, that feels good," he murmured.

"Yeah, it does." She gasped, appalled at what she'd said. "I love massages," she quickly added. "I don't get enough of them." The fact that she'd never had one in her life was irrelevant since he didn't know any different.

"Guess I'm going to owe you one after this. Do you like them hard?"

"The harder the better."

He laughed. "I'm not touching that one."

"Good idea."

"Ah, right there." He arched his back and moaned appreciatively as she worked her thumbs around the base of his neck. "Can you feel that knot?"

"Are you kidding? I thought I found a lost borough." Amazing that she could joke when his musky scent had all but surrounded her. She wanted so badly to touch his skin. To feel for stubble along his jaw.

Why in the hell hadn't she asked him not to shave for a day or two? That slightly rough look would have had the judging editors drooling. They wouldn't be able to give her the cover fast enough.

"Are your hands tired yet?" he asked, his voice low and languid. "You can stop at any time."

"It's not my hands, it's my lower back. I'm standing at a funky angle."

"Damn, I'm sorry." He pulled away.

"No. It's okay." She gripped his rock-hard right bicep

and urged him back toward her. "I shouldn't have said anything."

The type of shirt he wore disguised just what great condition he was in, and she was reluctant to let go even after he leaned back. But he didn't stay put.

He stood and turned to her with spread hands. "I'm willing to return the favor."

"That's okay," she muttered. "I'd rather get back to work."

"Ah, that." He looked genuinely disappointed.

"Tell you what, after we're done I'll give you an even better massage."

Surprise flashed in his eyes before they gleamed with pure masculine interest. "I'm holding you to that promise."

Her heart pounded. My, oh, my, but wasn't she getting bold. "All right," she said, all business again, even though her pulse had gone completely nuts. "We'll try something different. Pose the way you'd like to see yourself."

"Me?" He snorted. "Well, I sure wouldn't be standing here."

She sobered at his abrupt change in attitude. Why he suddenly decided to be difficult she had no clue, but she was running out of time and patience. "Okay, where would you be?"

He hesitated, probably because she sounded so patronizing, and then his lips curved slowly as if he were deciding whether to play the game. "At home."

"Doing what?"

"Reading a book."

"Where?"

"In my den in front of the fire."

"Alone?" she asked, annoyed at how eagerly she wanted the answer.

"Does my dog count?"

She grinned. "Absolutely. What's his name?"

"*Her* name is Tofu."

"Seriously?"

He nodded. "Best female friend I ever had. She comes when I call. Keeps me warm at night. Always glad to see me when I get home. No bitching, pardon the pun."

She gave him her best Freudian look. "So how long has it been since you've harbored this dislike for women?"

"I like women fine. But the ones holding cameras make me a little nervous."

"Good, then the sooner you cooperate, the sooner you'll get rid of me."

He chuckled. "You remind me of my friend's little sister. Seth and I grew up together, and whether we liked it or not, Emily used to tag along sometimes. She was quick and never let me get away with anything. Couldn't charm that one." He shook his head, the fondness of the memory lingering in his eyes.

Madison forced a smile. The comparison shouldn't have stung. She was always the girl next door, or someone's little sister…basically a nonentity. It had never bothered her. Not really. So why now?

Damn it.

His smile started to fade, and she realized she'd missed the perfect photo op. The real Jack Logan. The boy from Nebraska who'd made good.

She. Was. An. Idiot. If she didn't meet her deadline she'd have no one to blame but herself for being so unprofessional. Besides, nothing he said or did was about her.

The curious look he gave her brought her to her senses, and in her best businesslike voice said, "Tell me about your climb to the top."

"This is the top?"

"Most people would think so."

"Yeah."

There she went again. Too curious. Too interested. Hard not to be, though, with the acerbic way he'd sounded. "Okay, if this isn't your ideal career, what would be?"

"The career is fine."

"But?"

He pursed his lips, his expression thoughtful. "Off the record?"

"Nothing we say or do here goes to print. Or is repeated." No matter how much Shelly tried to pry anything out of her. "I'm only interested in capturing your essence. Not just the celebrity but the man."

"That's reassuring."

"It's not like I'm gonna reveal your deepest darkest secrets. They're just photographs."

"Just photographs," he repeated flatly.

She shrugged. "It's not rocket science."

His frown deepened and disappointment flickered in his face. He stared at her too long. "I want to see your work."

Madison tensed. "Like I said—"

"Now."

She choked out a laugh. "Now?"

"Where do you live?"

"You've got to be kidding." Obviously, he wasn't, and her stomach clenched painfully. What the hell was going on?

"We'll get a cab. Be back in time to wrap up."

"Stalling isn't going to do you a bit of good."

"I'm not stalling. I realize we have to finish the shoot."

"Then can we please do that?" She didn't feel nearly as composed as she hoped she sounded. Something in his eyes told her he wasn't playing with her. His interest was genuine. She just didn't understand why.

He pushed a hand through his hair and exhaled loudly. "I really do want to see your work. But I understand you have a deadline."

"Thank you."

"I give you my word we'll finish in time."

Reassured, she sighed.

"Even if we have to spend the night." He smiled.

10

JACK HADN'T BEEN totally forthright. He'd already seen some of Madison's work. Her published work, anyway. He wouldn't have agreed to do the shoot otherwise—no matter what kind of pressure the network imposed. What good would beefcake or sloppy pictures do for his career?

He still hated the whole idea, but at least her work was good. He'd seen the celebrity shots. Jack personally knew a number of them and recognized that Madison had done an amazing job of capturing the different facets of their personalities in only a few photographs. She had a gift.

At first all Jack cared about was that she did him justice. But he liked her. Even beyond the physical chemistry that had taken him by surprise. Larry had been right. She was driven and ambitious, hungry for success, in the same way Jack had been early in his career.

Before he'd sold out for fame and money.

No, damn it. He hadn't sold out. That was part of the climb. You had to go along until you had enough power to call your own shots. The trick was not waiting too long. Not waiting until you had more at risk than you were willing to give up.

"You're not serious," she said, staring at him with those fascinating wide brown eyes. "About spending the night."

He dragged his mind back to the conversation. "If that's what it takes."

She moistened her lips, her brows drawing together to form a slight crease. "That shouldn't be necessary."

"I have no ulterior motive, if that's what you're worried about."

"Uh, no." She laughed. "Didn't even cross my mind."

"Ah, you probably already have plans tonight."

"No, I mean, well, yeah. Sort of." She groaned and stalked across the room to look out the window. "Tonight just wouldn't work."

"How about tomorrow night?"

She squinted at him. "You'd have to get up early Monday to do your show."

"I have Monday off."

"Oh." She seemed disappointed or maybe annoyed. "I have another assignment tomorrow afternoon."

"Right."

"I do."

He nodded, irritated with himself for showing he was put off with her lack of enthusiasm. "It was just a thought. No problem."

She gave him a wan smile. "I'm gonna humble myself again. Sheesh, twice in one day."

"You don't owe me an explanation."

"I know." She shrugged, and the problem finally dawned on him. "I'm gonna be really famous one day. And rich, but—"

"You aren't yet. I get it, and I applaud your optimism.

It's imperative you feel that way so the hard knocks won't get you down. Persistence often wins in the end."

She grinned. "Well, I'm that if nothing else."

"You're much more than that, Madison."

She blinked and then looked away. "The sky is incredibly blue right now. It would make a great background shot for the pool since it's glass-enclosed."

"Aren't you forgetting something?"

She gave him a blank look.

"The four stooges?"

"Oh." She laughed. "On second thought, maybe the pool isn't such a great idea."

He well and truly liked her laugh. "About spending the night, think about it. My treat." At her quick protest, he held up his hand. "I'll put it on my expense account if it would make you feel any better," he said, even though he had no intention of sticking his boss like that. "That's the least the network can do for pressuring me into this."

"Gee, thanks."

He smiled. "No reflection on you or your professional ability."

"I don't know." The glimmer of excitement in her eyes took the wind out of her words. "It seems unnecessary."

"Weren't you wondering what it would be like to stay in one of these suites 'for real'?"

Her eyes widened. "Do you know how much the suites cost?"

"Yes."

"Plus we'd need two rooms."

He didn't say anything at first, but then reluctantly nodded. No denying he wanted her. More than he'd wanted a woman in a long time. But he wouldn't push.

She moistened her lips, her tongue making a slow sweeping motion as if purposely trying to make him crazy. "We're not just talking about the shoot, are we?"

At the growing excitement she seemed unable to disguise, he sucked in a breath. "That's up to you."

She blinked, her mouth parting, before she abruptly turned away and went into full business mode, fiddling with her camera and then poking in her bag and withdrawing another camera, this one digital.

He said nothing, just waited patiently for her to finish. What was there to say? He'd basically admitted that he wanted to spend the night together. And he was pretty damn sure she did, too.

MADISON, WHO TOOK PRIDE in being early to any appointment be it professional or social, got to Shelly's Family Portraits with only five minutes to spare. She'd overslept after a night of tossing and turning, with intermittent dreams of Jack Logan that had been so deliciously naughty she could have easily stayed in bed the entire day.

He'd really thrown her for a loop with his suggestion they spend the night at Hush. It sure had blown the rest of the day. Her concentration had hung on by a thread and when she got home and looked at the sloppy digital shots she'd taken, she realized how much he'd gotten to her.

Of course all she could think about was whether she should or shouldn't sleep with him. Of course she wanted to. He was sexy and intelligent and not at all arrogant as she might have expected. The chemistry was certainly there. But she had to finish the shoot first.

That was only partly why she'd left him dangling yesterday. Why she hadn't given him an answer about spending the night yet.

She smiled to herself thinking about the expectant look he'd given her at the end of the day, and when she'd told him she'd get back to him the next morning, he seemed disappointed. But the truth was, she still wasn't sure that she wanted to cross that line. She was waiting for that magic moment when she knew that having sex with him was totally what she was supposed to do.

She sighed as she started to unlock the door and found it open.

Unexpectedly, Shelly, who normally took Sundays off, was sitting at the front desk leafing through the latest issue of *People*. She looked up with an eager glint in her eyes that Madison fully expected but dreaded nonetheless.

"Hey." Madison preempted the anticipated barrage of questions with, "I have a favor to ask."

"Whoa. Back up. You can't do that."

"I haven't even asked you yet."

"Girl, you know darn well what I mean." Shelly promptly set the magazine aside and leaned forward. "I want to hear everything. Every last teensy weensy detail."

"I have to get set up."

"I did that for you already." She got up and followed Madison into the back room. Not only had Shelly set up the wintry backdrop the customer had requested, but the place had been rearranged. The inventory of varying sized chairs even looked polished. "I didn't want to give you any excuse for not dishing up the dirt."

Madison sighed. "There is no dirt. What are you doing here, anyway? It's your day off."

"For goodness' sake, you know what I mean." She pursed her bright pink lips in that practiced pout that Madison had seen so many times it was almost a trademark. "I'm not lookin' for real dirt, just some juicy stuff."

Watching the older woman waiting excitedly, like an addict looking for a fix, Madison suddenly got a funny feeling in her stomach. She'd known Shelly for almost four years but it was as if she was seeing her for the first time. What she saw made her incredibly sad. The woman was lonely.

After living life as a big fish in a small pond, the darling of Circleville, Texas, had come to New York expecting to find the red carpet to stardom. But there were so many women prettier, more talented, more connected than Shelly, and no matter how hard she'd tried or how long she stayed in the game, she quickly found that whatever she had to offer, simply wasn't enough.

Shelly had little social life, no close friends to speak of, only this small studio and her tabloid magazines that she read with too much fervor. Using her day off to needlessly clean up the studio.

For her, persistence hadn't paid off.

The idea gave Madison a chill.

Hey, they were totally different personalities. Had different goals. And Madison was much more realistic in her expectations. She thought about Jack, about them spending the night at the hotel that evening, and nearly choked. Hell, she could hardly sleep thinking about the possibilities. Yeah, that was realistic, all right.

She smiled at Shelly, suddenly feeling more compassionate toward her. "Problem is, there isn't anything juicy to tell. Seriously," she added at Shelly's frown of disbelief. "He's totally gorgeous, which you already know, and equally nice and polite, but he isn't happy about doing the spread and I wish he were more cooperative."

She looked disappointed and not totally convinced. "Did you get what you need?"

"Not really. That's part of the favor I was going to ask. I need to develop what I've shot so far."

Shelly's eyes lit up. "So far? You're meeting with him again?"

Madison nodded, annoyed with herself for the slip. At least she hadn't mentioned tonight.

"When?"

"We haven't discussed that yet." Before the lie left her lips, she turned away to check the camera already on the tripod. "His schedule is hectic."

"I can help you develop them," Shelly offered.

Madison hesitated at first, but saw no harm. "Thanks. That would be great."

"I don't suppose that when you see him again you'd let me meet him."

"Shelly, you know better."

"Can't blame me for trying." She shrugged, her bright pink lips curving. "Give me the rolls and I'll get started while you take care of the Wilson kids."

Foolish how reluctant she was to give up the film. For a moment she thought about giving up the job instead. Let Shelly deal with the Wilsons. But the power bill was due next week and she needed the money.

She dug into her bag and handed over ten rolls. "I

don't expect to get them all done this afternoon. I just want to see how he's coming across."

Shelly's brows arched over her heavily made-up eyes. "Is there any doubt?"

"Like I said, he wasn't the most cooperative subject."

"I know you've looked at the digital shots already."

Madison nodded, hoping she wasn't blushing down to her toes. "Last night when I got home." She'd studied each one a dozen times until she could close her eyes and still see every detail of his perfect face. "They were okay. But I have to do better. Maybe there'll be a couple in this batch I can submit."

The door in front opened and she could hear the Wilson brood enter. According to Shelly, they'd been in once before and Madison had taken their family portrait, but she couldn't remember them. Good sign. It meant the kids hadn't been a problem.

"I'll get started on these," Shelly said, and quickly headed for the dark room.

Madison sighed, put on a happy face and went to greet her customers. Her smile faltered as soon as she saw the lineup of children. Five of them. All under the age of eight, she guessed.

"Hi, Mrs. Wilson."

The beleaguered-looking woman fisted a child's sleeve in each hand. "I'm sorry I'm late." She eyed the freckle-faced boy captured on her right. "We had a little incident on the subway."

"No problem. Which one of these little angels are we shooting today?"

"All of them."

"Great." Just *great*.

"Mom!" The freckle-faced boy let out an ear-piercing wail and tried to twist free. "Did you hear what that lady said? She's gonna shoot us."

"Tommy, be quiet. That's not what she meant."

"She's gonna shoot us?" one of the other kids asked with wide eyes before she started crying, too.

Madison put two fingers to her throbbing temple. Amazingly, above the noise, she heard her cell phone ring. She snatched it from her pocket and in the confusion, did something she never did. Answered before checking Caller ID.

Never mind. It was too late.

It was Jack.

JACK LOUNGED in his favorite burgundy leather recliner, stationed at precisely the right distance for maximum quality viewing from his sixty-inch, wide-screen television, and idly flipped through the channels.

He had it all. An apartment in Manhattan, a house in Connecticut, both professionally designed and customized to his every need or whim. He had a driver to take him anywhere he wanted to go, even Atlantic City or Washington, D.C., if the idea grabbed him. Tickets to any and all Broadway plays were his for the asking. So were invitations to the most sought-after parties on both coasts. He should be on top of the world. He wasn't.

Not that he lacked appreciation. But something was definitely lacking.

Today the television was on mostly for noise. Normally he'd be watching the other news stations, studying, analyzing. But his thoughts kept going back to yesterday. More accurately, to Madison Tate.

As if he hadn't already given her enough mental air time last night when he should have been sleeping. She wasn't going to be happy when she saw the dark circles under his eyes today. That is, if she ever called.

He looked over at the phone. What the hell? He grabbed it and let speed dial take over. Presumptuously he'd programmed her cell number into his phone last night.

"Madison?" It sounded like kids screaming in the background. Had he gotten the wrong number?

"Jack."

"Is this a bad time?"

"Well, yeah, sort of." The background noise quieted as if she'd walked away from it.

"Want to call me back?"

Her laugh was shaky. "That would be good."

"Okay."

She hung up without another word. Without appeasing his curiosity. Without reassurance. He took a deep breath and stared at the muted television. They couldn't be her kids. She would've said something if she had kids. Wouldn't she?

The phone buzzed and for a second he thought it might be her, until he realized it wasn't really the phone but the intercom. He answered the doorman, who had Larry downstairs wanting to come up.

Jack didn't particularly feel like talking to anyone, but Larry seldom visited, and anyway, he'd feel like a jerk if he refused. Grudgingly he pushed off the recliner and went to the door, opened it and headed back to his chair in the den.

Seconds later he heard the door close, but Larry didn't appear right away. Jack wasn't concerned. Knowing his friend, he'd probably stopped to help himself to a drink first.

Sure enough, scotch in hand, Larry entered the den. "You always leave your door open like that?" Larry stopped and stared before slowly sinking down into the adjacent sofa. "What's wrong with you? You look like hell."

Jack yawned noisily. "You came across town to tell me that?"

"It's noon. You haven't shaved. Your eyes are puffy and dark."

"You forgot to mention I'm still in my robe."

"What's going on?"

"Nothing. It's my day off. I'm relaxing."

"Right." Larry took a thoughtful sip of his scotch. "You haven't been drinking, have you?"

"Unlike you, I wait until a decent hour before imbibing. That is, when I think I can afford the indulgence without feeling guilty as hell."

"I thought you'd be in a good mood with yesterday being behind you." He muttered a curse. "Is that what this is about? You screwed up yesterday."

"Now, why would I do that?"

"Man, you are acting strange."

Jack sighed. "Yesterday went fine. I just have a lot on my mind." He contemplated the wisdom of asking, but he couldn't help himself. "You wouldn't happen to know if Madison has any kids."

"The photographer?" Larry reared his head back. "How would I know that?" He narrowed his gaze. "Why?"

"I just got off the phone with her and there sounded like a bunch of kids screaming in the background."

Larry tipped his glass back again, and then studied Jack with too much curiosity.

"What did you come over for, anyway?" Jack asked before the conversation went in an unwanted direction. He trusted Larry, often asked him for advice, but discussing Madison on a personal level seemed wrong somehow. Too private.

"To see how yesterday went."

"It was okay."

"She got what she wanted?"

"I don't know."

Larry frowned. "Tate didn't strike me as the kind of woman who'd leave a doubt."

He smiled at the fitting assessment of her. "That's about right."

"So?"

"We haven't finished."

"So that's why you're moping. How are you going to squeeze another session in?"

"I'm not moping. I'm pondering. And we're meeting later today."

"With you looking like this?"

"I know how to take care of the dark circles."

Larry paused, probably weighing the wisdom of his next question. With good reason. He wouldn't like the answer. But he'd ask nevertheless. "What are you pondering?"

Jack smiled. "My life. My career."

"One and the same, my friend. Best you remember that."

Jack lost the smile. He didn't need it rubbed in.

"You have only a week and a half to sign the new contract. I hope you've reviewed it."

"I've reviewed it." And he'd done some crossing out and made his own amendments. But he didn't want to get into that with Larry right now. For the first time in their professional relationship, they were on opposite sides of the fence. Larry would never understand and Jack didn't expect him to.

"So what do you think?"

"It's my day off, Larry." He got to his feet. "Catch me at the office on Tuesday."

"I don't like the sound of that."

"Don't worry. No surprises."

"Well now, that worries me. I was hoping you'd surprise me and finally see reason."

"Look, I don't have time to discuss this right now. Madison will be calling at any minute and I need to be ready."

Larry's face creased in a speculative frown but he said nothing as he pushed off the couch. He followed Jack out of the den and it would have been difficult for him not to notice the overnight bag Jack had packed and set near the coat closet.

Jack didn't care. In fact, good. Maybe Larry got the hint. Anybody who tried to reach him before tomorrow night was just gonna be shit out of luck.

11

"HI." WEARING JEANS again, a blouse and a cream sweater-coat that covered too much, Madison met him in the lobby, which fortunately was empty, or admittedly he wouldn't have stayed visible. Looking a little flushed, she had a small overnighter in one hand and her camera bag slung over her shoulder.

"Let me take that for you." He tried to reach for the overnight bag, but she shook her head.

"I'm good. Have you checked in yet?"

"Yep. Here's your key."

She briefly glanced around before accepting the plastic card.

He realized what it looked like, especially with her holding a piece of luggage. "I'm sorry. I didn't mean to embarrass you."

"I'm not embarrassed." She shrugged, her gaze searching his face, lingering on his unshaven chin. A small appreciative smile curved her lips. "I didn't want to compromise you."

That startled a laugh out of him.

Her eyes widened slightly and then she looked down at her hands. "I didn't see any paparazzi outside but— Anyway, I'm sure no one would think that you were with me."

"That's exactly what they'd think." He wasn't sure what she meant by that, but it didn't sound good. "I'm sorry I hadn't considered your privacy."

"Don't worry about it." She smiled and everything was okay again. "But if we do make the tabloids, make sure they think I'm a famous photographer."

He smiled back, but the comment pricked him like a needle. Probably meant nothing. But he'd been used too many times for publicity. "You have a tripod or any other equipment outside?"

"Nope. It's just you, me and the camera."

"You sure I can't carry that for you?" He tried to take her overnight bag again but she wouldn't let go.

"Trust me, it looks better if I carry it."

"Sorry, but my mama would roll over in her grave if she saw me walking empty-handed alongside a woman carrying a bag."

Madison had already headed for the elevator, as if she were going with or without him. "It's the twenty-first century. It's okay."

He absently pressed the up button. "That it is. Still hard to believe."

"Yeah, I know."

The elevator doors opened and he followed her inside. He used his key card for the penthouse floor. "What did you do for the millennium?"

She frowned. "Couldn't have been exciting. I don't remember. Oh, no, wait. I was at a party with my friend Karrie. Nothing special. What about you?"

"I worked."

"Really?"

"My choice."

"At the studio?"

"No, I was in Hong Kong."

She snorted. "Ah, gee, tough assignment."

He smiled. "Ever been there?"

"Hong Kong? The farthest I've been is Orlando. I went to Disney World twelve years ago with my parents and sister."

"I didn't know you had a sister."

She grinned. "Why would you?"

"Good point." He wanted to know about her. He wanted to see that damn navel ring again. "Does she live here?"

"Nope. Her husband got transferred to Los Angeles about a year ago. She wants me to go visit, and I will. But right now it's hard with work."

"With your job I'd think you'd be traveling a lot."

She gave him a wistful smile. "Someday I'll cover the globe. I hope."

He kept forgetting she was a freelancer and that money might be tight. It had been a long time since he'd had such worries. Granted, he now had enough money invested that he'd never be poor no matter what he did. But how much did he truly want to give up? That was the burning question. The one that sometimes kept him awake at night.

The elevator doors opened and he led her to the Westwood Suite.

She gazed at the black scripted name, her eyes wide and excited. "Ohh, I don't think I've seen this one yet."

"Good." There were only three suites available, and he was glad he'd chosen the right one. Glad he'd made her eyes light up like Times Square.

He opened the door and let her go in first.

She crossed the threshold and dropped her bag. "This is awesome."

He smiled and moved her bag to the side so he wouldn't trip over it. He left his, too, not wanting to disturb the moment. Right now he was enjoying her reaction too much.

He watched her walk around the room, touching the gold metallic drapes, the plush gold-and-black couch, and the frame of what looked to him to be an original Tamara de Lempicka, one of her portraits, with the geometric lines and golden Deco feel. "Someday when you're a famous photographer you'll be staying in suites like this all the time."

"I doubt it." She glanced over her shoulder at him with a wry grin. "I'm too cheap."

He'd thought that about himself once. Before he got used to a better lifestyle and didn't think about cost anymore. "Check out the television. State-of-the-art."

Madison laughed as she walked over to join him. "Spoken like a true man."

"What?"

"The most incredible artwork you could imagine, a view to die for and you notice the TV."

"So?"

She looked up at him, and the smile on her lips faltered. She tried to disguise her sudden discomfort by feigning interest in the television, but moving back a step only enforced it.

"I don't bite," he said, hoping to relax her.

His teasing had the opposite effect. She blushed, gave him a mischievous look and then blew his socks off by saying, "Too bad."

He hated that she'd taken him by surprise. A quick

comeback was needed to move things along. But he blew it when he couldn't think of a single witty thing to say, and she turned away.

Damn.

"I'm gonna go get my camera ready," she said, and went to grab her bag. "Which room is—?" She scanned the room, stared for a second at the only bedroom door and then narrowed her gaze on him. "Isn't there another bedroom or adjoining room?"

He slowly shook his head, keeping his eyes on her. "No such thing in this hotel. Remember, the place is entirely geared toward couples, not families, and I doubt they encourage orgies."

"Well, okay." She shrugged but couldn't hide her disappointment. "I don't live far. I'll go home tonight. No problem." She started to return her bag to its spot near the door, but he intercepted her.

"We have two choices. I can sleep on the couch, which I don't mind in the least. Or I can get a single room and you stay here."

"That's silly. I'll just go home after we're done."

Their fingers brushed when he pried the handle from her hand. He took hold of her bag. "Doesn't that defeat the purpose?"

Amusement sparkled in her eyes. "Which purpose is that?"

"Maximizing our time and meeting your deadline, of course."

"Of course." She eyed him for a moment before casting a longing look around the beautifully appointed parlor. "I could always sleep on the couch. I'm smaller. I'd be more comfortable."

"I let you haul up your own bag. Don't get carried away."

"You let me, huh? I guess I owe you a thanks." She studied the couch. "I think that's made of Chinese silk. Boy, I'd hate to mess that baby up."

"How? Do you drool in your sleep?"

"Only when I'm having a really good dream."

He chuckled and shook his head. Never had he met a woman quite like her. "There is another alternative."

Slowly she met his eyes. Obviously he'd said too much because she visibly swallowed. "Do I want to hear this?"

He refused to look away. "Only you can answer that."

"I absolutely won't be distracted."

"No," he agreed. "Work comes first."

She moistened her lips, swallowed again. "Speaking of which, we'd better get started."

He let the matter of sleeping arrangements drop. He'd sounded pushy. Not usually his style. But he had this deep-down gut feeling that after this weekend she'd slip away. Disappear. Go visit her sister in L.A., find a job and never come back.

The whole thing was ludicrous. All they had was a brief professional relationship. After tomorrow they probably wouldn't even give each other another thought. She was ambitious and talented and going places. He had more decisions to make than his brain could handle.

But none of that precluded tonight. She'd given enough signals she was interested and willing. He'd give her the shots she wanted. It wouldn't take long. Not when they both anticipated what was to come.

AFTER TWO AND HALF hours of shooting first at the pool and now the spa, Madison couldn't think of any one particular shot she'd taken that would ace the cover. She liked the slightly rugged look of his unshaven jaw, and she was truly grateful he'd made that concession, and she'd even captured a few really good candids, but he was holding back.

Not overtly. She wasn't sure if he even knew what he was doing. But he couldn't lie to the camera, and they just weren't clicking. And worse, she didn't know how to get through to him. How to get him to relax. How to get him to trust her.

Even more frustrating was the growing tension between them. She'd sworn she wouldn't allow herself to be distracted, but if she let her guard down for even a moment, her thoughts spiraled in a dangerous direction.

"Are you getting hungry?" Jack stretched just as she was about to snap one of those rare perfect shots.

"Damn it."

"What?"

She glared at him. "What do you think I'm doing with this camera?"

"Is this a trick question?" He gave her one of his high-priced megawatt smiles.

She didn't bite. Not even a little. She was too tired and quickly losing confidence. Never in her entire career had she needed to take so many rolls of film, and with so little yield. Thankfully a couple of shots from the garden had made the cut. But she was far from the finish line.

What really put icing on the cake was that the day couldn't have been more ideal. The hotel was quiet.

Only one person showed up at the pool, swam a few laps and then disappeared. Other than an employee, they had yet to see anyone at the spa. They should have been making terrific headway. They should have wrapped up already.

She sighed and rubbed the tension tightening the back of her neck. This feeling of discouragement was new to her. She hated it. She hated feeling out of control. She totally hated the idea of not getting that cover.

Jack sobered, his eyes darkening with concern. "Seriously, I think we should take a break. Maybe get some dinner. It's about that time."

"Want to get serious? Then start paying attention to what we're doing here."

Confusion flashed across his face. Along with a touch of anger. "I've done everything you've asked."

"Yes, you have. Just like a good little robot."

He frowned and looked as if he wanted to say something, but nothing came out. He really didn't get it.

"How many times have you looked at your watch in the past hour?"

His lips thinned. "I haven't the faintest idea."

"You're just putting in time. You don't care about—" She stopped herself. Her emotions were too close to the surface, and she was likely to say something she'd regret. As if she hadn't already stuck her big foot in it already. She didn't need to make him mad. "You're right. Let's take a break. Go get something to eat."

"What about you?"

"I'm not hungry." She forced a smile. "Go have dinner. Take your time. We'll work later. I wanted to get some nighttime shots, anyway."

He stayed where he was and stared at her. "You're angry. Tell me why."

"I'm sorry for overreacting. I really am. It's not you. It's me."

"Right."

"It's true. You made it clear from the beginning that you didn't want to do this. I thought I could make it work." She took a couple of deep cleansing breaths, hoping it would calm her, but instead the brief time-out gave her temper time to spark.

"No, I take that back. You share the blame," she said, not caring that his face darkened. "I could have made it work, except you won't give an inch. I know you can't understand how important this is to me. But it is. It's huge. This is the biggest break I've ever got. I need this win."

"'Could have' made it work?" He gave her a patronizing look that fanned the flames. "Funny, you didn't strike me as a quitter."

"You're the one who quit. Before you even started. You accepted my reassurance that I'd keep the spread tasteful. You pretended to give me the benefit of the doubt, but it was only lip service. You didn't come through."

"I don't know what you want from me."

"Yes, I think you do. It's what you want from me I'm not sure of."

He winced. "I like you, Madison. It wasn't and isn't my intention to let you down. Maybe you simply want too much."

"Maybe." She drew in a deep, shuddering breath and

turned away hoping he hadn't seen how emotional she was becoming. "Go have dinner. I'll be in the suite." If she stayed, she would use the bedroom. The hell with him. "We'll try again later."

She kept going without a backward glance.

JACK SAT ON THE EDGE of the hot tub and watched her go. He felt as if a tornado had descended and then left just as quickly as it had appeared, leaving a big mess behind. No rhyme, no reason. It just was.

She was off base. He'd cooperated. Wasn't staying the night his suggestion? It wasn't just about the sex, either. Yeah, he had designs on her, but he wanted her to meet her deadline. He hoped she got the pictures she wanted. He wasn't crazy about being on the cover, but he hadn't sabotaged her in any way.

At least not consciously.

He thought back over the past twenty-four hours and got a little uneasy. One of the things you learned early on when doing live TV was to school your face in a neutral expression. To not let your feelings show or get in the way of your reporting. It wasn't so different from acting. You let loose only what you wanted the audience to see.

He sighed and dropped his chin to his chest.

Okay, so he hadn't been the model subject. Maybe he'd held himself in check at times. But consulting his watch often was a habit. He did it all the time. At least he'd been up-front about not wanting to participate. She had to give him credit for that.

He wouldn't be able to take it if she was sitting in the suite crying. She didn't seem the type, but her eyes had been awfully glassy before she left.

Damn.

"Mr. Logan?"

He looked up and a pretty blonde, unnaturally tanned for this time of year, dressed in skimpy black shorts and Hush's trademark pink T-shirt was standing before him.

She smiled. "Are you waiting for a massage?"

"No, I'm not."

"Would you like one?" She shrugged a shoulder that called attention to her generous breasts. Not that he hadn't already noticed. "I don't have another appointment for a couple of hours."

The idea tempted him. He was tight and knotted all over. And his appetite had vanished, so dinner held no appeal. But the image of Madison's bleak face and watery eyes stayed with him and he didn't want to risk letting her out of his sight for too long.

"No, thanks," he told the masseuse as he got to his feet.

He and Madison had unfinished business.

MADISON LAY across the bed in the most beautiful room she'd ever been in, which she should be enjoying but was totally miserable, and tried calling Karrie for the second time. Again no answer.

Just as well. Madison hated bothering her just to bitch. If she hadn't found Rob it would be different. In the old days, when Karrie was single, they used to call each other for every little thing. No matter what time it was or how silly the reason. Madison missed those days.

She let the cell phone drop onto the luxurious satin comforter. The rich fabric must have cost a bundle, and it occurred to her she shouldn't be lying on it like this. But at least she'd kicked off her shoes.

Staring at the ceiling, she sniffed a couple of times, but so far she hadn't let the tears come. Wouldn't happen. Even when she was totally hormonal she wasn't the weepy type. Besides, as ticked-off as she was with Jack, she wasn't through with him yet. He owed her a cover. And she was gonna make him pay up even if it took all night.

Just for the heck of it, she thought about trying Karrie again, and then just as quickly discarded the idea. Karrie and Rob had been away from Vegas for quite a while and probably had errands to run, catching up to do. Or maybe they'd simply unplugged the phone while they made mad, passionate love for hours.

Madison groaned and rolled over to bury her face in her hands, careful not to get makeup smeared on the satin. She wasn't jealous. Not of Karrie. Not really. It was all Madam Z.'s fault.

She chuckled at her own irrationality and then sighed. She still didn't believe in the psychic's power, but *if* there were anything at all to the woman's supposed gift, why hadn't Madison been as lucky? Why hadn't she met the man of her dreams?

Jack came to mind. Well, theoretically she supposed she had, but she meant a viable candidate. Not someone untouchable. Not someone who was only interested in a one-night stand. Or at least he had been. By now he probably couldn't wait to get rid of her. She doubted he'd stay the night. She would, though. No way was she passing up this opportunity. Besides, what else did she have to do?

Oh, she was a first-class idiot. She hadn't gotten laid in so long. And she could have been with Jack Logan. Now, she *was* ready to have a good cry.

She fumbled for the cell phone. Just one more time she'd try Karrie.

A knock at the closed bedroom door startled her.

"Yes?"

"Can I come in?" It was Jack.

She quickly sat up and smoothed her hair. "It's unlocked."

He walked in, holding a bottle of bourbon in one hand and two glasses in the other.

12

"I THOUGHT YOU WENT to dinner," she said, scooting off the bed and then remembering her cell phone. She stuck it back into her pocket.

"Am I interrupting?"

"Nope." She watched him walk to a table by the window and set down the bottle and crystal tumblers and then pour about an inch of the amber liquid into each one. "A Sunday dinner tradition?"

He said nothing, didn't even smile, but carried both glasses across the room and handed her one. "Let's talk."

"Bad idea." She took a small sip and felt the liquor burn all the way down her throat to her very empty stomach. "We did that. It didn't work."

"Can we sit down?"

"Do anything you want." She immediately regretted the caustic edge to her voice.

He didn't seem to notice or chose not to. He smiled. "That's quite an offer."

She shook her head in mock disgust. Tried not to smile back but couldn't help it.

"I'll start by apologizing."

She took another sip, nervous suddenly about what was to come. "I'm sorry, too. I shouldn't have said—"

"I'm not finished. You were right. I've been taking this matter too lightly."

There were no words that wouldn't sound spiteful or petty, so she just folded her hands together and listened.

"I've been selfish, trying to skate through this and only thinking of my own interests." He gulped down the rest of his drink. "My contract is coming up for renewal and, according to my agent, my agreeing to do this is a bargaining chip."

"For more money?"

He laughed.

She cringed. "Sorry. None of my business." But what else could it be? He had everything. A top-rated show. A couple of awards on his shelf. An adoring public. She waited for him to continue, curious at his sudden hesitation.

"Money isn't the issue," he said finally. "I want to spend some time reporting stories as they're happening, wherever they're happening." His mouth curved in a self-deprecating smile. "And as you so succinctly put it, I don't want lip service from the network. I want it in my contract."

"That seems simple enough."

"Believe me, it's not." He shook his head with a grimness that furthered her curiosity. "I'm not trying to make excuses. This isn't even about me. This is your career, and it's no more fluff than my morning show. They both serve a purpose."

"Fluff?" She didn't know whether to be more indignant about the insult to himself or her.

"I said it *wasn't* fluff." He went back for the bottle, poured himself more and then took the bourbon to her.

"But you did have to deny it."

"Christ, Madison, don't make this more difficult."

Surprised that she'd finished her drink, she held her glass out and he filled it halfway. "Okay, you're right. I won't overanalyze."

"Thank you." He took her hand. "Let's go sit down."

She nodded and let him lead her into the dimly lit parlor, really glad he'd brought the bottle with him. Especially when he sat right beside her on the long, deep couch, so close their thighs touched.

"Are you drunk?" she asked, suddenly wondering how many he'd had before now.

"No. You saw me have my first one."

She decided she'd better set the glass aside and pace herself. The bourbon was definitely taking effect. The only thing she'd had to eat was a candy bar around noon.

He leaned toward her, lifted her chin and touched his lips to hers. He retreated just as quickly, leaving her baffled, and a little angry.

"What was that for?"

"Because I've wanted to kiss you since yesterday."

"You call that a kiss?"

He smiled. "I call that not wanting to get slapped."

"Chicken." She cupped the back of his neck and pulled him toward her. He came readily and their lips met clumsily at first. But quickly he took control, slanting his mouth over hers and greedily consuming her.

Heat surged through her like an inferno. Her nipples tightened and she squeezed her thighs shut, afraid of the dampness already pooling between them.

She pulled away, struggling for breath. "I can't believe I just did that."

"Sorry?"

"Nope."

"Problem is, it wasn't enough."

"No?"

He shook his head while his gaze stayed steady.

She grabbed a fistful of his shirt and pulled it free from his waistband as their mouths met again.

"Wait," he said unevenly against her mouth when she slid her palm up his belly and into a thatch of soft hair.

She stilled her hand, embarrassed, ready to withdraw.

"There's something else I've wanted to do." He tugged up the loose hem of her blouse and stared.

"What?" She looked down, confused.

He shifted on the couch, then lowered his head and peered closely at her navel. "What is this?"

"Don't tell me you haven't seen a navel ring before."

"This one's different."

She laughed softly. "It's got a couple of diamonds strung through the hoop."

"Real ones?"

"God, no. I've lost two already."

He smiled a wicked smile, still leaning over her thighs. "How?" He stuck the tip of his tongue through the hoop, grazing her navel at the same time. "Like this?"

She shivered. His head rubbed against her breasts as he took the hoop between his teeth and lightly tugged. She arched her back and his hands came up under her shirt, his palms sliding up her skin to cup her breasts.

"You're not playing fair," she whispered, as he used his thumb and forefinger to tease her hardened nipples through the silky bra.

"How's that?"

"Take off your shirt."

He smiled. "Take off yours."

"Together."

"Okay," he murmured against her skin, his beard-roughened chin slightly prickly and giving her goose bumps, and making no move to release her.

She let her head fall back, wondering if she should pinch herself. This couldn't be real. This had to be another one of those dreams that kept waking her last night.

He swirled his tongue around her navel and then started to travel up toward her breasts.

She stopped him. "Your shirt?"

He let out a grunt of frustration, but sat back and unbuttoned his shirt. As more and more skin was exposed, she could barely keep from touching him, keep from running her fingers over the ridges across his flat belly. Keep from exploring more of the silky hair that fanned out between his brown nipples.

"Come on. You, too." He stopped unbuttoning to run a thumb down her cheek and then slid it across her lower lip. "You're so soft."

She swallowed hard. This was totally real. And she had to be crazy. But she didn't care. She yanked off her shirt, and then helped him unfasten his last button.

"Your bra, too," he said hoarsely.

She slid one strap off her shoulder, and he took care of the other one. Her gaze went to the window. The drapes were still open. They were high enough up to be safe from prying eyes, but it was still disconcerting.

He reached for the front clasp holding the silky cups together but she stopped him and glanced significantly at the windows.

"No one can see in."

"Still."

"No problem." He got up, and she watched him walk toward the window, sorry he hadn't already taken off his shirt. But the return trip gave her a great view of his perfect chest, and she got all tingly knowing she was about to explore every inch of it.

She waited until he'd settled next to her and she was pushing his shirt off his shoulders, then asked, "Why didn't we just stay in the bedroom?"

"Believe it or not, I truly intended to talk." He shrugged out of his shirt and let it fall behind him.

"What happened?" As if she had no say, by their own volition her hands immediately went to his chest. Slowly she dragged her palms over the peaks and valleys of sinew and muscle.

"I lost my head." His eyes closed briefly, his chest rising and falling unevenly beneath her hands. "But it's your fault."

"How so?"

"You look so good I couldn't keep my hands off you." He unclasped her bra and roughly pushed the cups aside. Her nipples ached from being so tight for so long, and as if he knew, he tenderly, reverently stroked each tip with the lightest of touches.

She moaned softly, and he smiled, his eyes so dark with desire they were almost the color of milk chocolate. He pushed the bra straps off her shoulders, and when she shrugged back to help release them, he dipped his head and touched his tongue to her nipple. The cool dampness on her fevered skin sent a shiver down her spine, and she closed her eyes, praying this wasn't a dream.

She opened them again just as he brought his head up, and the pure male beauty of his face stole her breath. "Why are you doing this?"

He drew back, frowning at her, the dazed look in his eyes lingering incongruously. "What kind of question is that?"

"I want to know."

He blinked, his eyes clearing, and she was a little sorry she'd broken the spell. Maybe he'd come to his senses. Get dressed. Leave.

And did she really want to know? Or did she want this one glorious time with him more?

"It's pretty obvious," he said, amusement in his voice as he trailed a finger between her breasts. "You're a beautiful, intelligent, spirited woman."

Madison gasped softly. "Don't say that." She didn't want to hear his spiel, the one he used on every other woman he'd been with, except with them it was probably true. "Really. You don't have to."

He looked genuinely confused. "You asked."

"I know." She had the sudden urge to cover herself. "Okay, I am pretty intelligent and unquestionably spirited."

He cocked his head to the side, searching her face, his expression speculative and not especially pleased. "Don't do that, Madison."

"I'm not in your league. We both know that."

"Ah." One eyebrow went up in challenge. "What exactly would this league be?"

She decided not to answer. Anything she said would probably make matters worse. Instead she reached for his belt buckle.

He forced her chin up. "Are looks the only thing that interests you?"

"Of course not."

"Then why give me so little credit?"

"You're twisting things around."

"Beauty comes in many forms. So does ugliness." He cupped one of her breasts in his hand and gazed down at her pearled pink nipple. "This is beautiful," he whispered, and lightly brushed it with his lips.

He transferred his attention to the other one, again touching it lightly with his lips. "Exquisite."

He looked up. "Your eyes, your lips, your smile…all beautiful. All a part of you."

The sincerity in his eyes was almost more than she could absorb without coming apart at the seams. She leaned in and kissed him hard, pulling his belt loose.

He had the zipper to her jeans down equally as fast. And in seconds they were both free of clothing, her pink lacy panties lying atop his brown silk boxers on the expensive Vivienne Westwood rug.

Anxious to see him, all of him, she urged him to lean back against the couch. It was too difficult not to stare, so Madison just gave in and looked at his lap. The hard length of his cock lay heavily against his belly, incredibly and fully aroused. It had to be. Any bigger and…

Shuddering, she touched the velvety tip where a bead of moisture had already formed. He twitched, and she wrapped her hand around the base, fighting the temptation to lick him clean, taste his saltiness.

He moaned, his eyes fluttering closed for a second. Touching her wrist and applying a little pressure, she knew he wanted her to release him, but she wasn't ready.

His lips curved in a lazy but knowing smile. "Hey."

"Hmm." She stroked upward.

"Oh, no." He took her wrist and pulled her away, forcing her upward. "Come here."

She crawled over him, his cock pressed against her skin, forging a path between her breasts, down her belly as she slid up to meet his lips.

He moaned, his hips moving beneath her, grinding, his sex pressing against her mound, and he kissed her hard. His tongue parted her lips, touched hers, and then dove deeper, sweeping the inside of her mouth, exploring every spot.

Madison's whole body trembled as his hands ran down her back, settling underneath her buttocks. He shifted her so her knees straddled his hips, so that she was spread open and ready.

Her hands bracketed his shoulders, balancing on the back of the couch and as she got used to the position she gasped when his cock head left a slick trail over her lower belly.

All the while he hadn't stopped kissing her. His scratchy stubble would leave her marked, but that was the least of what he was doing to her. She could feel how much he wanted her, and not just the thick evidence that strained to be inside her.

His kiss, his kneading hands still cupping her bottom. She pulled back to catch her breath. To look once more into his desire-darkened eyes. His hands inched closer together and she gasped as his fingertips brushed her inner folds.

"Madison," he whispered, all hoarse and gravely.

She'd never heard him like this. He was completely

different from the man on television, from the man she'd photographed. This was the real Jack Logan. Strong, sexual, not in the least politically correct.

He lifted her, his arms cording, the muscles in his neck straining, until she was posed atop his cock. She took the hint and took over, more to see what he would do next than to give him a break.

What he did was worth it. Holding his cock, he rubbed her clit, gently at first, and then more forcefully. She breathed hard, and grinned as his gaze shifted to the lift and fall of her breasts as if mesmerized.

"Are you gonna play with that all night, or you gonna get on with it?"

His mouth dropped open and he looked at her face again. A few seconds later he chuckled, although he never stopped teasing her. "You think I'm just playing at this?"

She nodded slowly.

"Oh, really?"

She arched her right eyebrow. "See? Even now, it's talk, talk, talk."

"You're a real badass."

"Bad as they come."

His grin grew more wicked as he trained his cock to rub in hard, small circles, just where it would drive her the most crazy. "Which means you'd never, ever be reduced to begging."

She inhaled deeply, arching her back. She knew it would bring her nipples closer to his mouth. She'd seen the way he'd wanted to taste her. To turn the screw even deeper, she leaned forward, so her breasts were millimeters from his lips. If he'd reached with his tongue, he could have lapped the hard buds. "Me? Beg? Never happen."

"Well, that's good to know," he said, his breath brushing her sensitive flesh. "I wouldn't want to ruin your image."

"My image?" she said, trying to control her voice, to not give away how close she was to coming. "You should talk. Does the network have any idea who you really are, Jack? Do they know that they can never tame you?"

His lips parted, and she heard his sharp intake of breath. "They don't have a clue," he said, as he grew completely still.

She bit back a moan, but she couldn't control the way her thighs gripped his hips.

Again, he laughed, so low it was almost a growl. "You think I'm untamed, do you?" His left hand went to the curve of her hip where his fingers dug into her skin. "You ain't seen nothin' yet."

He thrust up with his hips, impaling her completely as his hands forced her down.

She cried out as her head fell back. Her hands moved from the couch to his shoulders, and she knew she had to be hurting him, but she didn't care.

His teeth captured her nipple, holding her still while his tongue flicked rapidly, sending incredible sensations from her breast straight down to where he filled her.

Both of his hands were now on her hips, he lifted her slowly, until just the tip of him was inside her. She tried to move down, but he wasn't having any of that. His teeth tightened just enough to remind her that she was in no position to argue.

Only when she whimpered did he fill her again. But

he took his time about it. The only thing she had to use were her inner muscles, and she used them without mercy.

It was his turn to moan. His eyes practically rolled back in his head as she squeezed him harder still.

She bent her head down as far as she could, as close to his ear as possible. "Beg me," she whispered.

"No," he said, although the word was almost all breath.

She released her muscles, waited until she felt him quiver insider her, then she squeezed again. "Do it."

He pulled her up, but this time there was no teasing. She came off him, lifted high by the strength of his hands, and an instant later he thrust up and brought her down. It was explosive and raw and she howled as he did it again and again. And then she was coming, moving her hips in tight circles, making him gasp and curse until he was coming, too. Pushing, pushing, until they were both suspended and her heart couldn't beat any faster.

They collapsed together, her body falling across his, their panting breaths the only sound in the quiet of the night. For a long time, that's all they could do, just try to get some kind of equilibrium. And then she heard his voice, a whisper close to her ear.

"Ready?"

13

MADISON AWOKE FIRST, one leg thrown over Jack's, his arm around her shoulders. At least, she thought she had until she moved her leg and his eyes opened.

"Hi." He smiled and squeezed her shoulder.

She snuggled closer, and his arm tightened around her. "How long have you been awake?"

"A few minutes."

"We're in the bed."

He nodded.

"How did that happen?"

This time he chuckled. "Magic."

That sounded right to her. She yawned. "What time is it?"

"You don't want to know."

"Uh-oh." She tried to turn over to see the bedside clock, but he hugged her to him and kissed her, starting with the tip of her nose and then capturing her lips.

She allowed him to distract her with his tongue and probing fingers, but only for a couple of minutes, until she noticed a ribbon of sunlight curling under the drapes.

"It's morning?" She twisted around to look at the clock. "Good God, it is morning."

"Yep." He nuzzled the side of her neck, his chin deliciously rough against the sensitive skin below her ear.

Of course, not an inch of her wasn't sensitive after last night. The man was thorough, if nothing else. She didn't think there was a spot on her he hadn't kissed or licked or sucked. He was energetic, too. Had her using muscles she hadn't used in forever. If ever.

She sighed contentedly, even knowing she was in deep trouble. Ten rolls of unused film sat in her bag. She couldn't think of a single shot she'd taken yesterday that thrilled her. Oh, any picture he took was good. He was blessedly photogenic. Equally good-looking in print as he was in person or on television. But she still hadn't captured that sparkle. That one unidentifiable, elusive quality that made a photograph stand out from the rest.

"Shall I order up some coffee?" he asked, his fingers doing wickedly wonderful things to her nipple. "Or would you rather stay in bed for a while?"

She laughed when, at the same time, he slid his other hand down her belly, his finger brushing the tiny strip of hair at the juncture of her thighs. "Now is that a fair thing to do?"

"Yes."

"You're not supposed to answer a rhetorical question."

"You're not supposed to laugh when I'm trying to get romantic."

She propped herself up on one elbow. "That's not romantic. You're just trying to get laid again."

Laughing, he fell back against the pillows, one arm flung across his forehead. "You are something else."

She smiled, and slid back down again, pressed up to him, and placed her hand on his chest. "Guess what?"

He looked at her from under his forearm, his brows dipping dejectedly as if he already knew what she was going to say.

"We have to get back to work."

"I know," he said, but he didn't look happy. "Can I have another kiss first?"

"You can have a dozen if you want." She started at his collarbone.

"I want," he whispered hoarsely when she got to his left nipple, and then worked her way down his belly, stopping to tongue his navel.

She flipped the sheet off him, and sucked in a breath at how huge and hard he was already. How was she supposed to get out of bed now? At this point, she didn't think she'd remember how to use a camera.

This wasn't good.

He reached for her, and hauled her up to suckle her breasts.

Then again, this was very good.

JACK SCRATCHED his bare chest and then leaned toward the mirror. Amazing he didn't have ugly, dark, half circles under his eyes. If he'd gotten three hours of sleep last night he'd be surprised. And given the chance, he'd do it all over again.

Madison had been everything he'd expected. Even more. The woman's energy level astounded him. Thrilled him. Charged him with a vigor he hadn't possessed since he was in his early twenties. He'd be ready for several more rounds if they didn't have to get up. But as hard as he'd tried, he hadn't been able to talk her into forgetting about shooting today.

It wasn't as if he were trying to get out of it. Now that he'd gotten past his self-absorption, he fully understood how important this was to her. He simply didn't want whatever magic they'd conjured to end. Because it would soon enough. That was inevitable.

Her ambition was both admirable and annoying. So was her single-mindedness. If she hadn't fought so hard against the chemistry that had been brewing since yesterday, he might have suspected she was like countless others. Using him in their climb. But not Madison. Not when she looked at him with those soft brown eyes. Not when she smiled at him, a special smile meant for him alone.

He wrapped a towel around his waist, finger-combed his wet hair and then left the bathroom in search of her. She'd gotten out of the shower first, anxious to go check the lighting in the parlor. Her desertion hadn't offended him. They'd already been in so long their skin had shriveled. Which, she'd pointed out, did not make for good photos.

She wasn't in the bedroom, but her digital camera sat on top of the nightstand, so he picked it up as he continued into the parlor. The camera was small, easily concealed in his palm as he found her, sitting on the couch in a black lacy bra and matching bikini panties, loading her camera.

She looked up and gave him one of those special smiles. "I ordered coffee."

"And food, I hope."

"Nope. If you're hungry we'll go down to the restaurant." Her gaze flickered to his chest, and she drew in her lower lip, quickly looking away. He knew then that if he wanted, he could play dirty. "You know very well what'll happen if we stay up here."

"And your point is?"

She shook her head, returning her attention to loading the camera. The bra was one of those skimpy ones that allowed her breasts to mound high over the lace. "What happened to work first, play later?"

"Who said that?"

"How quickly we forget."

He took advantage of her preoccupation and glanced at the digital camera. Fortunately, it was the same brand and similar to one he had. While she still wasn't looking, he raised the camera and focused.

"Madison?"

She looked up.

He clicked. Her mouth opened in outrage and he clicked again.

"Hey!" She stood. "Give me that thing."

He got off two more shots.

"You are in so much trouble, buddy." She made a grab for the camera but he sidestepped her and kept clicking.

He grinned. "What? Don't you like having your picture taken?"

"No, as a matter of fact." She almost snatched it, but he held it up high over her head. She was tall, but not tall enough to reach, and she poked him in the ribs.

He grunted but held his ground. "Let's look at them and then we'll erase them."

She pursed her lips in disgust, and then walked away, the black panties hugging her rounded backside and making his heartbeat quicken.

He chuckled. "Don't get huffy. It's your camera. These pictures aren't going anywhere."

And then he saw what she was up to, and took a step back. "Not funny."

She'd picked up her other camera. Facing him, she aimed and said, "Say cheese."

"Madison." Panic swarmed him. A tabloid picture of him standing in only a towel flashed before his eyes.

She grinned but there was no flash, no click. "Trade you cameras."

"Okay, you win." He walked toward her with the camera in his outstretched hand.

She lowered hers, a hint of disappointment in her face. She knew that in that instant, faced with the camera focused on him, he hadn't trusted her.

But what did she expect? So he was gun-shy. He had every right. Every reason. She had to understand that.

He looked into her eyes as he handed her the digital camera and saw no disapproval, no resentment, and realized she did understand. She'd respected his fear. She hadn't taken the shot. And just as he had a right to be wary, she had the right to be disappointed. Already it was over.

And Madison was smiling again.

Something inside him swelled. Threatened his air passage. Made him warm inside and out. He looked down at his arm to see if it was flushed with color. It looked normal.

Still, he didn't feel normal. He didn't even know how he felt. Off balance. Short of breath. Confused. Definitely confused.

"Are you okay?" She touched his arm, her eyes warm with concern.

"Yeah, I'm fine." He shoved a hand through his hair. It had started to dry. "I'd better go get dressed."

"Don't worry. I won't take a shot until you're ready."

He eyed the digital camera still in her hand and then met her eyes. "Go ahead."

She blinked. "Really?"

"With the digital." So he was a little chicken. "I want to see it first."

She hesitated. "Okay." After setting the other camera aside, she checked the digital and then brought it up to focus. She moved closer and snapped, and then lowered it to look at him. "May I take a couple more?"

"Go for it." He knew he'd been tense, that the shot probably stunk. He drew in a breath, let it out slowly, forcing himself to relax.

She took another step closer, and he focused on the way her breasts lifted, gauged just where her perfect pink nipples were behind the black lace.

So involved with studying the way her breasts rounded above the bra like two small melons, he barely noticed the flash. But it must have come because she moved to a different position.

She crouched, balancing herself with one knee to the floor, the other bent as she sat on the heel of her foot. "Look off to the right," she said, and then gestured with her free hand when he didn't obey.

He couldn't. Fascinated with the length of toned muscle that ran up her thigh to her crotch, his gaze stayed glued to her leg. To the smooth hollow where her leg joined her pelvic bone.

The flash went off and broke the trance.

He blinked at her.

She stared back, over the camera. Awareness crackled in the air between them. She moved and had to brace herself with her free hand.

He didn't dare go help her. She was fine. But one touch and there'd be no guarantees.

"Um." She noisily cleared her throat and gestured with a jut of her chin. "You don't want me taking a picture like that, do you?"

He looked down. The towel had tented. He muttered a curse.

Madison laughed. So hard she lost her balance. She saved the camera but landed on her backside. His attempt to grab her arm made him lose the towel.

She wasn't laughing anymore. She stared, blatantly, with such raw desire he didn't hesitate lowering himself over her. The bra and panties disappeared and then there was only skin rubbing skin, slickness sliding into slickness, lips hungrily meeting lips.

And then nothing else mattered.

AMUSE BOUCHE was crowded. Lots of people in business attire having power lunches. Or pretending to. There was far too much ogling going on for Madison's taste. People you wouldn't expect to be so rude or obvious thought nothing of staring for long unsettling moments.

Not at her, of course. But at Jack. Although she did get her share of curious glances. Once they realized she was nobody, they tended to transfer their attention to Jack.

Poor baby. No wonder he was camera shy.

The thought reminded her of this morning, and her pulse started to race. She'd gotten some fantastic shots before they'd ended up on the floor like a couple of teenagers in heat.

Nothing she could use without him flipping out, but she'd keep them forever. Until the photo paper was so old it disintegrated. Astonishingly, he hadn't asked her to delete them. Not yet, anyway.

"Hey, Logan, where were you this morning?"

Jack smiled at the rude, twenty-something man passing their table. "Even I get a vacation day now and then."

Madison growled softly and leaned forward so no one but Jack could hear. "If one more person asks you that question, I am definitely going to pluck every one of their lashes out. Slowly. Painfully."

He chuckled. "Remind me not to piss you off."

"And you thought staying here for lunch would eliminate some of that crapola."

"I'm so used to it, it doesn't bother me anymore." He glanced around the restaurant. Only one vacant table remained. "Let's make a bet. I say we'll hear that at least three more times before lunch is over."

"Seriously, I don't know how you stand it." She leaned back when the waitress appeared with their meals. A shrimp salad for Jack that was awfully pretty but wouldn't be enough to fill one of Madison's cavities.

In front of her, the waitress set down a burger topped with caramelized onion slices, bacon and blue cheese, and accompanied by *frites,* which was just a fancy name for shoestring fries so they could double the price.

"May I have another cherry cola, please?" she asked the waitress.

"Another mineral water for me," Jack said, and then shook his head as the waitress left.

"What?" She cut her burger in half.

He eyed the juicy medium rare meat with longing. "Give me part of that burger, huh?"

"Don't you like your shrimp salad?"

"I'm sure it'll be fine, but I want some of *that*."

She bit into one of the crispy fries and smiled. "What would your personal trainer say?"

"That I'm bigger and much stronger than you, and that you'd better do as I say."

She laughed, loud enough that several people turned to look. She put her head down, cleared her throat and then looked up at him. "I'll give you half. But only because then I'll have room for dessert."

An eyebrow went up. His eyes glittered with meaning. "You want dessert?"

"Want me to drop this burger?" She smiled and passed him the plate. "You can't have any of my fries, though. I draw the line there. You want some, you have to order them."

She wasn't in any better shape than he was. Everything south of her chin had twinges of aches and pains. Dormant too long, or overused, she wasn't sure why. She only knew she'd had one hell of a workout. Four times counting this morning. And if he made the slightest overture, she'd be ready in a heartbeat.

He took a bite of the burger, chewed for several seconds and then laughed for no apparent reason. After he'd swallowed, he said, "I was just thinking about the upside of field reporting. No personal trainer breathing down your neck. The down side is that most of the places you end up, you couldn't get a meal like this not even for a thousand bucks."

"What do you eat when you're way out in the desert or jungle?"

"MREs just like the military." At her blank look, he added, "It's the new name for rations—Meals Ready To Eat. New name, same bad taste."

She made a face.

"You don't mind. Not when you're in the middle of the action. So much happening all around you, your adrenaline rocketing so high you don't care much about anything else." He looked out toward the sidewalk, past the people rushing to or from lunch. His mind was far away, wrapped around some fond memory he hadn't shared. "You're right there, right in the middle of history being made."

"It does sound exciting," she said, and he looked back at her as if he'd forgotten she was there, as well. She took no offense. She understood, even appreciated his fervor. That kind of passion was something everyone deserved. At least once in their lifetime.

"I'll show you some footage of me reporting the Gulf War." He shrugged, looking somewhat embarrassed. "If you want. No big deal."

"I'd love to see it." Her heart thudded. Was he kidding? He'd all but said he wanted to see her again. "In fact, I think it's only fair you do, if you want to see my work."

He grinned. "Deal."

"Deal."

They continued to eat and talk, as if they'd met years ago instead of just last week. It got to the point where she barely noticed the stares. But when they were almost done, a woman and her daughter approached him for an autograph, and Madison watched him graciously abandon his lunch and take the pen.

She wasn't sure she could be as cordial. They could've waited until he was done eating. But she didn't say anything, didn't even smile when the woman gave her a curious look.

Instead she finished her fries, battling anger that so many people seemed to think Jack was public domain. Were they raised by wolves, for goodness' sake? How could he stand it? Everyone seemed to want a piece of him.

Including her.

The unwelcome thought made her stomach roil. She pushed it aside. Their relationship was different. Professionally, the idea was that they mutually benefited. Personally, she wanted nothing from him. At least, nothing more than he wanted from her.

As soon as the woman and her daughter left, Jack said, "Sorry about that."

"You don't need to apologize. These people and their lack of manners appall me."

"Now that's something I won't miss."

"What do you mean?"

"When I'm out in the field."

"Yeah, but you've gotta come back sometime," she said wryly.

The way he avoided her eyes stirred her curiosity.

"You are planning to stay with the morning show, right?"

"I don't know. Probably. Like I said, I'll be signing a new contract soon." He winked. "So who knows?"

"Don't look now," she said, watching two women who'd apparently spotted them and actually come off the street hurrying through the open restaurant in their direction. "But I think you're about to get assaulted for another autograph."

"Ah, hell." He quickly signaled the waitress for the check. "We'd better get out of here. I assume you have more shots to take."

"Oh, yeah."

Madison watched silently as he courteously signed autographs for each of the women and listened patiently about how they were from Nebraska, a town not far from where he grew up. She only half listened while mentally replaying their earlier conversation. The passion in his voice echoed in her head. He wanted back in the field. No doubt about that. And he had no intention of coming back to the morning show. He may not know it yet. But she did.

14

MADISON SAT at the head of her double bed, her legs drawn to her chest, arms wrapped around them, taking up as little room as possible, afraid to move for fear of disturbing the dozens of photographs of Jack she had laid on the bed. The rest covered the cheap tan carpeted floor, her tiny oak dresser, the bulletin boards nailed to her walls.

But she didn't want to use the larger sparser living room like she normally would. Couldn't bring herself to share any of these yet. She had two roommates, one a flight attendant and the other a buyer for Macy's. They each had weird or busy schedules and rarely saw each other, which worked out great. But tonight of all nights, Bethany was home.

So Madison had hibernated with all her treasures surrounding her. If someone walked in on her, she'd easily be accused of stalking. Jack's face was everywhere. Smiling Jack, brooding Jack, playful Jack and her favorite…Sexy Jack.

Her gaze drew to the one positioned at the foot of her bed. Propped up slightly, she immediately found his eyes, lion's eyes, dark golden with such raw and feral desire, her heart pounded. His lips were ever so slightly parted, his full lower lip nearly three-dimensional and his jaw and chin shadowed with stubble.

She'd taken that photograph of him in the parlor suite as he gazed down at her. Her! He was looking like that at her. Madison Marie Tate. Holy Moly.

She hugged her legs tighter, closed her eyes, remembering that day less than a week ago as if it were happening now, as if she could feel his mouth on her lips, his palms cupping her breasts, his cock driving into her, hard, fast, furious. She opened her eyes, barely able to catch her breath, and there he was in front of her, stealing every ounce of common sense she possessed.

What was she going to do? She knew exactly which pictures she should submit. The one that would surely win her the cover. That was painfully obvious. But could she? And it wasn't just about him. In fact, because of his hectic schedule, she hadn't seen him since the weekend, but he'd called three times and not once asked about the pictures.

Of course, she knew which ones he'd veto if asked. And they had a deal. But that wasn't even her dilemma. She'd created her own problem. Yeah, she still wanted the cover. But did she really want it as badly as she had before?

She gazed again at the picture at the foot of her bed. This was her Jack. The man who'd ignited something in her she hadn't known existed. It didn't matter that their relationship was fleeting. He'd secured a place in her heart forever.

Did she really want to share that Jack with the world?

"BRING ME A CUP of black coffee, would you, sweetheart?" Larry said, presumably to Lana, before he entered Jack's office and closed the door.

"Christ, Larry, don't call her sweetheart."

"What?"

"And get your own coffee. I get mine."

Larry stared at him as if he'd grown an extra nose. "Aren't we chipper today?"

He sat in a leather chair across from Jack's desk, automatically patting his breast pocket for his cigarettes, even though he knew he couldn't smoke in Jack's office. That meant he was nervous. Jack didn't blame him. The older man wasn't going to like what he had to say.

"All right, give me the bad news first." Larry slumped in the chair, his jowls sagging like a basset hound's.

No sense sugar coating it. "I have two changes I want made to my contract."

Larry sighed heavily. "Tell me it's for more money. They'll give you more money."

"You know better."

"Yeah, unfortunately."

A brief knock at the door preceded Lana's entrance. Smiling, she carried in two mugs of coffee and set them on the desk in front of them.

"Thanks, Lana."

"No problem."

"See?" Larry immediately picked up his mug and winked at her. "She doesn't mind."

"Lana, do me a favor," Jack said, and she stopped expectantly at the door. "Next time this guy asks you for coffee, tell him to get it himself."

Battling a smile, she wordlessly let herself out, closing the door behind her.

Larry muttered a mild oath. "With the mood you're in, I'd rather discuss this another day, but we're running out of time."

Jack looked him sternly in the eye. "There's no discussion. I want a fifty-fifty split."

"What? Fifty percent of your time away reporting stories?"

Jack nodded.

"You're crazy. They won't go for that. They won't even go for twenty."

"And I don't want them sending me to Paris to cover Bastille Day or to London for the Queen's birthday. I want real assignments. The grittier the better."

"Jack, read my lips. I'm telling you they won't do it. No way. Forget it."

He stiffened. The hell he'd forget it. Maybe he wouldn't get the fifty, but he wouldn't settle for less than forty. "Maybe they have a new anchor in mind."

"You're not serious." Larry looked pale and shaken. "Come on, have you stopped to think about how much you have to lose?"

Jack nodded solemnly. He'd thought about little else for the past week. With the exception of Madison. He'd thought a lot about her, too. Maybe too much. Not just about the sex, which was beyond incredible. Her passion had inspired him. Reminded him of how he used to feel about his work. How he needed to feel again.

That didn't mean he wasn't concerned, even a little scared. Larry was right. He had a lot to lose. But he had more to lose if he didn't go for it. He'd be lost himself.

MADISON ANSWERED her cell phone, her pulse already starting to pick up speed. She knew it was him from the Caller ID.

"Hey," she said casually and hurried to the dark room for privacy and quiet. The client hadn't arrived yet, but Shelly was reading one of her tabloids out front.

"Good morning."

The deep timbre of his voice never failed to send a shiver down her spine. For some reason it sounded more seductive on the phone. Which didn't make sense, unless it was because on the phone she wasn't distracted by his beautiful hazel eyes or his muscular chest.

"You sound as if you just woke up."

"I'm hurt. You obviously didn't watch my show today."

"I taped it. I'll watch it later."

He laughed. "Right."

Little did he know that was the absolute truth. All week she'd been taping the show each morning and watching it at least twice, skipping commercials and segments that didn't include him. She was nuts. Certifiably. She didn't care.

"I was wondering if you were doing anything tonight?"

She smiled. "What do you suggest?"

"Dinner."

"Eating is always good."

"My place?"

"You're cooking?"

He chuckled. "I wouldn't do that to you."

"I'm a takeout kind of gal myself." Actually, a candy bar or two made a great lunch, a granola bar when she got disgusted with herself and tried to be healthy.

"I have a better idea. Let's meet at Hush."

"For dinner?"

"We'll stay there, spend the night in one of the suites and order room service. Tomorrow's Saturday. I don't have to get up early."

"That's crazy." She cupped her hand over the phone, hoping Shelly hadn't heard her voice go up a couple of octaves.

"Why?"

"It's way too expensive."

"I make a lot of money, remember?"

"Show-off."

"You know better." His voice lowered. "What good is money if I can't spend it on someone I care about?"

She bit her lip, thrilled at his words, but struggling not to give it too much weight.

"Anyway, this will be a kind of celebration."

"For?"

"I'll tell you tonight."

She heard commotion out front and knew her clients had arrived. "I have to go."

"Tonight then?"

She hesitated. Of course she was going to see him. But it seemed like such a waste of money. Still, she couldn't exactly ask him to her place...

"Come on, Madison," he said coaxingly, "aren't you curious about the toy chest?"

Her breath caught. "What time?"

JACK WAITED FOR HER in the bar, the one where they'd first met. The place was crowded with Manhattan's beautiful people, being Friday afternoon and Hush being the hot spot of the hour. Fortunately, a couple of popular stage and screen actors were also there, so at least Jack wasn't bombarded for autographs or small talk.

However, a blond woman who looked barely old enough to be in the bar had approached him when he first sat down. She'd been annoying and pushy, and he politely told her he was waiting for someone. After that, it didn't take long for her to lose interest.

He took a sip of his scotch, checked his watch and glanced over his shoulder hoping Madison would be early as usual. It was hard not seeing her all week, harder than he'd anticipated. He'd talked to her every day, though, and three times today. Each time he'd remembered something else he needed to tell her. Surprisingly she hadn't, in true Madison fashion, told him to get a life.

Someone bumped into him from behind and, annoyed, he turned around. It was Madison. She gave him a funny look, reared her head back and said, "Do I know you from somewhere?"

A couple sitting next to him looked over in amusement.

He shook his head. "Uh, no, I don't believe so."

"Hmm, I could've sworn we'd met before." She planted herself on the stool he'd saved for her. "Buy me a drink while I mull this over."

The couple's gazes locked in amazement, and the woman looked as if she were about to spit out her drink.

"What would you like?" Jack wouldn't have minded playing along, but he wanted so badly to kiss her. So he did. A brief touching of lips, mostly friendly, nothing nearly satisfying, but enough that her eyes widened and color blossomed in her cheeks.

"Um, do you think that was wise?" she whispered,

sliding the couple a worried glance. They'd caught on and returned to their own business.

"Did I embarrass you?"

"Of course not. I was thinking of you."

"Screw 'em," he whispered back, a second before he kissed her again. This time he lingered, tasting the peach flavor that coated her lips.

She broke contact first. "For a guy who didn't want his picture taken in this hotel, you sure are pushing the envelope."

He had to laugh. "You're right. Look what you've done to me."

"Me?"

Not quite ready to tell her this was his first step in asserting his independence, he simply smiled. And then he bumped his leg on something and looked down. It was her briefcase. All by itself. He frowned. "Where's your overnight bag?"

"Everything's in there," she said, indicating the briefcase with a nod of her head.

"Everything?"

"You said we're having room service." Her lips curved in a teasing smile that managed to be sexy as hell. "I figured I didn't need to bring much. And a briefcase is so much less telling."

He caught her meaning, and a warmth spread throughout his chest. Her concern wasn't for herself but for him. "I hope you made room for the photographs I asked you to bring."

She nodded slowly. "I brought eight of my favorites just as you wanted. I also brought a dozen I took of you. The final cut, so to speak."

"Good." He'd been trying not to think about those. He wasn't sure if he wanted to see them. What he did want was for her to get that cover she was convinced she needed. And she was right. Being awarded a cover for *Today's Man* would be a major career boost.

The bartender took her order while Jack's thoughts had taken a detour, and he was sorry he hadn't asked her if she wanted to go up to the suite instead. Of course, that would have defeated the purpose of asking her to meet him here. He didn't want her to think their relationship was only about sex, or that she was his dirty little secret, good for behind closed doors but nothing more.

"When did you get here?" she asked, turning to face him, her denim-covered legs bumping his knees. She started to move them but he put a hand on her thigh.

He didn't want her angling away. He liked looking at her, liked getting lost in her warm brown eyes. "I got to the hotel about half an hour ago, got checked in, took my stuff up and then rushed down here about ten minutes ago trying to beat the crowd." Glancing around, he saw that few tables were left and nothing at the bar. "Happy hour starts earlier than I remember."

"Fridays tend to be like this. Everyone seems to get a half hour head start on the weekend." She cocked her head to the side and gazed thoughtfully at him. "You get up so early, I guess your happy hour starts at about noon, huh?"

"Yeah, right."

"What do you do after the show?"

"Research, pretape interviews, phone interviews, prepare for the next day, that sort of thing."

"When do you nap?"

He smiled. "I go to bed early instead. Pretty boring, huh?"

She grinned back. "I thought all you celeb types partied the night away."

"Not morning-show staff. You might try in the beginning but you learn quickly that four in the morning comes damn fast." He recalled his early days, young and brash and full of himself—he'd tried to do it all, any A-list party and he was there.

"Of course it has nothing to do with getting old."

"Definitely not." He gave her a mock glare. "What do you do in your free time? Besides visit psychics."

Her glare was genuine. "Hilarious."

He started to laugh and then a crazy thought struck him. "Do you think she was talking about me?"

"Who?"

"Madam Zora."

Her martini arrived and she quickly took a sip, glancing sideways at him. After a longer sip, clearly not keen on discussing the subject, she put the glass down and started on her olive.

He snorted. "You thought about it, too."

"That's ridiculous. You know better."

He didn't know what to believe. "Come on. What you told me… It's not so far out there."

She shoved her hair back with a shaky hand and moistened her lips. "Do you know how crazy this sounds?"

"Yeah, but it's possible. There is evidence that some people have a kind of sixth sense. The police and FBI have used them. Who's to say Zora isn't one of those people." He paused, fascinated with how nervous she was getting. "Her accuracy is the reason she's become so popular."

She drew in her lower lip and stared at her glass, "I don't know. "It's just that— I don't know."

"I'm the closest person to a coworker you have, right?" He gave her some space, let her think for a few moments before voicing his suspicion. "She said something else, didn't she? Something you don't want to tell me."

She hesitated. "It didn't make sense. I barely remember what she said."

"Tell me."

"She said something about me embarking on a great adventure." She laughed. "Me, a girl who's never been west of the Hudson River."

The prophetic words chilled him to the bone. Tore a hole right out of him. God, he hoped Madam Zora was right. But now wasn't the time to get into it with Madison. It took him a few seconds to trust his voice. "Hungry?"

"Always." If she thought it odd he'd dropped the subject so quickly, she didn't show it.

"After we finish our drinks how about we go upstairs, order some dinner—or appetizers for now if you're not ready for dinner yet. We do have all night."

A sultry smile curved her lips. "I'm counting on it."

He couldn't finish his scotch fast enough while signaling for the bartender so he could pay the check and they could get out of there. The guy saw him and nodded, but before he presented the bill, the blonde who'd approached Jack earlier came and squeezed in between Jack and the long-haired man wearing a Stetson on his left. The cowboy didn't seem to mind. Jack did.

He angled more toward Madison, giving the blonde

his back, but she touched his arm, her red-tipped fingers lingering too long. As tempted as he was to ignore her, he knew his best course of action was to see what she wanted, and then politely refuse.

Without a word or even a smile, he glanced over his shoulder at her.

She leaned in close, her hand was back on his arm, and he had to really hold on to his temper. "I didn't realize this was a business meeting."

"Who said it was?"

The woman's gaze flickered to Madison. She briefly wrinkled her nose as if confused, and then smiled. "Anyway, I didn't mean to disturb you. I just wanted to give you this."

Before he could stop her, she slipped a piece of paper into the breast pocket of his sport coat. He looked at Madison, but couldn't tell if she'd seen it.

"Call me, okay?" The blonde slipped away, but not before rubbing her large half-exposed breasts against his arm.

Normally, that kind of crap annoyed him. But for the woman to have done it in front of Madison really made his blood pressure soar. Not that she was the kind of woman who cared. She'd probably find it funny, knowing her. But it was the principle, damn it.

The bartender delivered the check and Jack pulled out some cash. He finally had the guts to look over at Madison, who was taking her last sip, appearing to be oblivious to what had just happened. Breathing a sigh of relief, he laid down a large bill and got to his feet.

"Ready?"

"You don't need change?"

He shook his head and picked up her briefcase. It wasn't heavy. She clearly hadn't packed many clothes. Heat blazed in his chest. Down lower in his groin.

Man, how he'd thought about her all day. All week. And now she was right next to him, leaving her stool, her mouth a breath away from his as she rose. He wanted to kiss her. Really kiss her. Thoroughly. Right in front of everyone. The hell with them. Let them talk. Let them take all the photographs they wanted.

But he wouldn't do that to her. Madison would be hounded and photographed for a week. She'd hate it. She might hate him.

He ushered her ahead of him, letting her take the briefcase when she insisted. Just in the half hour he'd been there, the bar had grown obscenely crowded. Good. People paid him less attention. Which made more sense when he caught sight of Piper Devon at the entrance, surveying the room.

He stopped briefly to say hi and to introduce Madison, and then they continued toward the elevator. Just as the doors opened, he fished out the piece of paper with the blonde's phone number and dropped it into a trash receptacle.

15

MADISON SAW HIM DROP the piece of paper in the trash can and her heart leaped. If he hadn't, it would have been okay. He was a free agent, and the woman was drop-dead gorgeous even if she did have fake boobs.

But he had done it, and he was here with her, Madison, who'd always been the tallest, skinniest girl in class all through high school, who'd waited for a prom date who never showed up, and who was about to spend the night with Jack Logan.

Again.

Once had been faboo enough. But twice? And he'd done the asking. She was sorely tempted to do the happy dance. Right here. Right now. Outside the Carnaby Suite. But he'd think she was a nut, and why blow things now.

She swallowed hard and turned to him with a smile as he slid the key card in and then pushed open the door.

"Does this meet with your approval?" He swept a hand for her to follow into the suite. The drapes were open, and fading sunlight bathed the room in a surreal pinkish-golden glow.

"Oh, I think it'll do," she said imperially, but couldn't hold back a laugh at the last moment.

"May I take this now?" He took the briefcase from her.

"No peeking."

He didn't go far. He set the briefcase on the floor, wrapped his arms around her and hauled her up against him. Taken by surprise her breath caught in her throat when he covered her lips with his, sending her head back with the fierceness of his kiss.

She stumbled a little and he held her tight, slowly releasing her mouth. He tipped her chin up and ran the pad of his thumb across her cheek, across her lower lip. Kissed her again, softly this time.

"Sorry, but I waited a week to do that."

"Me, too," she admitted, while fisting two handfuls of his shirt and forcing him back to her mouth.

He readily complied, and there was no sound in the room, in the entire hotel but the low guttural moan that came from his throat as he parted her lips with his tongue and darted inside, taking her on a wild ride that she wished would go on forever.

But his cock was hard and insistent against her belly, and she had other plans for him. She pushed his sport coat off his shoulders, and he quickly got rid of it. Beneath he wore a white cotton shirt woven so fine it felt like silk as she ran her palms up the front, over his hardened nipples.

"I thought you were hungry," he whispered.

"I am."

He smiled and yanked her shirt from her waistband. It was one of her nicest blouses, silk and expensive, a gift she'd received from Karrie last Christmas. The thought occurred to her when her attempt to unfasten the top button sent it flying across the room.

They both tracked the motion, and then she saw

them. A basket of bright spring flowers sat on the table. They didn't look quite right, though.

She squinted at them. "Are those—?"

"For you," he said, the amusement in his voice stirring her curiosity.

She abandoned him and moved closer.

"Hey, where are you going?" He laughed, knowingly, and followed her across the room.

As soon as she got closer she started laughing, too. "They're cookies."

"My trainer would be appalled."

"Hmm, my kind of cookie." She lightly touched the orange-glazed petal of what was supposed to be a mum. Incredible workmanship.

"I figured you might enjoy these more than flowers." He came from behind and wrapped his arms around her, resting his chin on her shoulder.

The gesture was so warm and familiar, as if they'd been lovers for years, that she shuddered with pure contentment.

He drew back. "What's the matter?"

"Nothing." She aligned her arms over his, squeezing lightly, urging him to stay where he was. "They're just too pretty to eat."

"Take one bite and tell me that."

"That good, huh?"

He murmured something, but his mouth was pressed against the side of her neck and she didn't get it. Didn't care, either.

She closed her eyes and let him, with his lips and tongue, minister to her skin, her earlobe, the curve of her neck. All her senses rose to a fever pitch. Thrummed to an awareness she didn't know she possessed.

Maybe Madam Z. was one of those people who saw things others didn't. Maybe she had been warning Madison about Jack. Maybe he was the one who'd take her to the apex. The one who would irreparably break her heart.

Why had she been so stubborn? Why hadn't she let Madam Z. finish the reading?

"You're tensing," he whispered against her skin. "What's wrong?"

It didn't matter. None of what the psychic said did. Madison had been right to begin with. The whole prediction thing was schlock. She had to forget it. Enjoy the moment. Enjoy tonight. Because this was all she was gonna have.

"Nothing," she said, turning around to bury her face against his chest and breathe in his unique and mysterious scent. His top two buttons were unfastened, and the hair on his chest tickled her nose. She giggled.

"What?" He lifted her chin, and he was smiling and that was all she needed.

And then someone knocked at the door.

JACK FROWNED when he heard the room service waiter identify himself. He looked questioningly at Madison but she shook her head and shrugged.

He hesitated a moment, willing his arousal to go down, not be so blatant, and then opened the door to a guy bent over a silver ice bucket, rearranging a bottle of Perrier Jouet that sat on a white linen tablecloth. Beside it were a tray of chocolate-covered strawberries, both white and dark and a dozen pink roses.

The man smiled and straightened. His nametag identified him as Tyler. "Compliments of Piper Devon."

Jack stood aside while Tyler pushed the cart into the suite, fishing in his pocket for a suitable tip.

"Anywhere in particular you'd like me to set this up?" the waiter asked.

Jack looked at Madison. Her untucked blouse and wild hair was a pretty damn good indication as to what they'd been doing.

She shrugged. "Right there is good."

This was Hush. Tyler was obviously unfazed by what went on behind closed doors. "Would you like the champagne opened now?"

"No." Madison spoke up quickly. "Thank you." She gave him a hint by moving toward the door, her arms crossed over her chest, a trace of cream-colored lace showing where the blouse parted slightly over her breasts.

Tyler looked questioningly at Jack. He smiled and opened the door. He really liked that she didn't defer to him. She had a preference and acted on it. He liked that a lot. Of course, so far, he liked pretty much everything about her.

"Have a good one, sir, ma'am." As the waiter left, Jack handed him a twenty, and then double bolted the door.

"I don't care who knocks," he said, walking toward her. "No more interruptions."

She met him halfway. "I totally agree."

"Except when we order dinner."

She nodded and slid her arms around his neck.

He felt the weight of her breasts pressed against his chest. "*If* we order dinner."

"If," she agreed, and nibbled at his chin.

He ran his palms down the slender curve of her back

to where her backside rounded, and he filled his hands with her offering. His cock responded, pressing hard against his fly. She undoubtedly felt it, too, and he silently berated himself for going so quickly. For forgetting that he had a plan for tonight.

With regret he pulled back, missing her heat, the way her fingers lightly clawed his back. But he knew once he started running his palms over bare skin, once he tasted the honey between her thighs, there'd be no more talking. No more rational thinking.

Or at least not how he'd planned.

He smiled into her confused face. "I didn't have lunch."

She blinked. "Oh."

"That scotch is getting to me."

"Have a strawberry."

"I think I'll need something a little more substantial than that."

"Okay." She seemed disappointed as she moved back. "Order something from room service while I have a strawberry."

"Madison." He caught her wrist as she turned toward the room service cart. "You forgot something."

"What?"

He tugged at her arm until she was up against him again, their lips melting together, their tongues mating, their bodies pulsing to the same beat. It was harder this time to release her, but he did, while he was still capable of seeing the bigger picture.

She smiled, looking more reassured, as they both moved apart. He went to the desk and picked up the room service menu, and she headed for the cart. After deciding on a couple of appetizers, he punched in the right number.

Madison strolled leisurely toward him, nibbling the chocolate off a strawberry. She bit into the fruit and then put it to his lips. He had time for one small taste before someone answered.

But she didn't back off. Instead she played dirty while he tried to give their order, licking the corner of his mouth, running her palm down his chest, tucking her fingers into his waistband.

The woman on the other end of the line must have thought he was insane. Or drunk. The way he could barely get out each word. She already knew who he was and, thanks to Hush's sophisticated phone system, had greeted him by name.

Ordinarily the distraction would have aggravated him. That is if any other woman had engaged in this behavior that resulted in him sounding like a fool. But not Madison. She only made him want to get off the phone and carry her into the bedroom. Lay her across the bed. Strip her naked. Maybe even see how the infamous fur handcuffs in the armoire worked.

He finally got the order in and hung up. "You are in so much trouble."

"Yeah? Oh, my. I'm scared." She laughingly pushed the last bite of strawberry between his lips.

"You licked off the chocolate," he complained with a mock frown.

"Poor baby."

He touched her breast, quickly found the hardened nipple with his swirling forefinger. She gasped with pleasure. "You're going to be sorry you started this," he said, taking satisfaction in the way her eyes drooped closed.

"I truly doubt it."

"Even when room service knocks again?"

Her eyes opened. "Oh, that."

He chuckled, and with no small effort, lowered his hand. He was anxious to see her work. Although he doubted there would be any surprises. "How about we go explore your briefcase while we wait?"

"Really?"

"We have to sometime."

She gave him a sultry smile "Says who?"

"You're bad."

"I try my best."

"Come on." He took her hand, grabbed the briefcase where they'd left it near the door and then led her to the couch.

The coffee table was more for show than anything else adorned with attractive art objects, which he cleared away before setting her briefcase on top.

"Wait a minute. It's locked." Sitting beside him, she leaned forward to release the combination, her fragrant almond-scented hair teasing his nostrils, distracting him, frustrating him.

He drew in a deep breath, reminded himself they had all night. The thought alone sent his mind spinning in the wrong direction. He forced his attention back to her flipping open the top. The first thing he saw was a red lace teddy. And groaned.

She looked at him. "You don't like it?"

His laugh sounded strangled. "I like."

"Oh." She took it out and laid it on the black lacquer

table. Next came a pair of skimpy bikini panties. "For tomorrow," she said, before removing them and the white T-shirt beneath.

A small black bag, probably makeup, and a leather portfolio was left. His gaze stayed on the folder, and he took the liberty of reaching for it while she set aside the small bag.

"Hey. Those aren't your pictures," she said, relieving him of the portfolio. "There they are."

"I didn't think they were." He stared down at the manila envelope that had been hidden under the portfolio. Did he want to see them? No matter how they turned out, he wouldn't stop her from submitting them.

"Don't you want to see them?" She picked up the envelope when he made no move to do so.

"Maybe I should wait until they're in *Today's Man.*"

Her eyebrows rose and her lips parted in surprise. "You still have veto power. Although I don't think you'll find any of them objectionable."

"I trust you," he said, and glanced at the leather portfolio. "I'd like to see those."

She didn't move, only stared at him as if she wasn't sure what to do. Finally she unclasped the folder and drew out several eight-by-ten photographs. "I just brought a few from my private collection," she said, not meeting his eyes and looking uncharacteristically shy. "They're ones I just shot on a whim. No big deal."

He reached for them, but she held back the stack, removing several and keeping them hidden before turning the remainder over to him. If she thought he was going to forget about them, she was out of her mind. She'd really piqued his curiosity now. "Am I allowed to see those?"

"Later." She smiled tentatively. "I promise."

He nodded, sat back and started with the first one. He immediately recognized Central Park. Sitting on a bench, an older woman, either a nanny or a grandmother, was being fed a bite of hot dog by her young ward. The expressions on their faces were priceless, the affection between the woman and child nearly a tangible thing.

"This is terrific," he said, carefully setting the photo aside and going to the next one. Again, taken in Central Park, this one black-and-white, showed what appeared to be a homeless woman, frail and battered, feeding the birds part of her sandwich.

The tender expression on the woman's face stirred a fierce emotion in him that words could never have done. He looked at Madison. Her hands were clasped together, tightly enough to make her knuckles white, her eyes wary, almost frightened.

"Madison."

"What?"

"These are fantastic."

She smiled, halfheartedly, as if she thought he was voicing only what was expected.

"Do you have any idea how good these are? Have you shown them to anyone else?"

She shrugged sheepishly. "My friend Karrie."

"And was she totally blown away?"

She laughed softly. "Of course. She's been my best friend like forever."

"No, Madison." He took hold of her chin to make her look at him. "Not because she's your friend. These are fantastic. They should be in a gallery somewhere. In a magazine."

She snorted. "People only want to see celebrities."

"Not true." He let her go and went to the next photo. "You're wasting your talent."

She seemed to shrink away, and he let her have her space while he studied the next four, all equally as powerful as the first two. He wasn't biased. He'd had enough friends and family hit him up for endorsements over the years to know whether he could be objective or not.

No, she had a remarkable talent for capturing universal human emotion. That was crystal clear. Even the last one, humorous as it was, displayed her talent and quickness. A squirrel sat on the gas tank of a motorcycle, its paws strategically resting on the handle bars.

Jack smiled.

"That was a really lucky shot," she said, having leaned closer again. "I couldn't believe that little guy perched up there big as life."

"Didn't you submit it anywhere? You could've easily made a few bucks off this from *Parade* or one of those mags."

"I sent some out a couple of times and got rejected. Like I said, people are more interested in celebs." She took them back and stuffed them into the envelope.

He got the feeling she wanted them out of sight. Forgotten. "You should be very proud of every one of those photographs."

She smiled, shrugged. "I've enjoyed them."

Frustrated, he checked his watch, wishing room service would hurry up and get here, then leave. She really didn't understand her own talent. And he had a feeling nothing he could say to her would change that.

Damn, maybe she really did need that silly cover for

validation. The thought truly irked him. But as talented as she was, he didn't doubt she would get the prized cover. And if that's what she needed to boost her confidence, so be it. He was simply relieved that she was as good as he'd anticipated. Better even. It would make his proposition easier.

"What about those other pictures?" he asked, indicating with a tilt of his head, the stack she'd secreted away.

"More of my private stuff."

"I know that. I want to see them."

She made a face, clearly reluctant, but then produced them. "Remember, no one else will see these."

He frowned, but as he started through the small pile, he understood. These were the photographs she'd taken of him; the ones when he'd come out of the shower, wrapped only in a towel. She'd been careful not to advertise the fact he was undressed. The first two shots showed only his bare chest, as if he might have had on a pair of jeans or swim trunks. But that wasn't the attention grabber, anyway. It was his expression. As he looked at her.

There was no doubt as to what was on his mind. *Sex* might as well have been tattooed across his forehead. The feral desire in his eyes made him look almost primitive. He tried to remain expressionless, but panic simmered in his chest. Quickly he flipped through the others. They weren't quite as bad, but he barely recognized himself.

"I'd like to keep them," she said quietly, "with the promise they're for my eyes only. But if you confiscate them, I'll understand."

"Confiscate?" He snorted. "Trying to make me feel guilty if I do take them?"

She stiffened. "That's not at all what I meant."

"That was a joke. Here. They're yours." He was damn lucky his hands didn't shake as he handed them over. Not because he was angry, just startled. Dumbfounded. Kind of annoyed that he'd been so transparent.

He'd give just about anything to have been inside her head when she first saw the photos, saw the animal lust in his eyes.

An awkward moment passed, and then he said, "You aren't submitting those?" It was a question, not a demand.

She gave him a cheeky smile. "Would you want me to?"

He didn't say anything.

"Don't worry. I already have my five choices tucked away."

"In the envelope, right?" Now, he was interested in seeing them.

"Yep."

He smiled and leaned toward her.

"Later," she said, taking a last glance at his photograph and sliding her arms around his neck.

16

AS MUCH AS SHE'D DREADED showing him his photographs, she couldn't in good conscience not give him the chance to keep them or destroy them or do whatever he pleased. It would have broken her heart if he hadn't let her keep them, and not just because he would've deprived her of many hours spent drooling. That he trusted her meant everything in the world to her.

She smiled with the deepest contentment she'd known in a long time as she watched him answer room service's knock. It was Tyler again, one hand splayed beneath a tray carrying a couple of silver-domed plates. At Jack's request, he set them beside the cookie bouquet, and then nodded at her before quickly disappearing.

Ignoring the food, Jack returned to join her on the couch.

She smiled lazily at him. "I thought you needed to eat."

"It wasn't the scotch getting to me." He slid one of her buttons free and then another until the front of her bra was exposed. "It's you."

"You're gonna make me blush," she teased.

"I see that. It's starting right here." He insinuated his finger between her breasts, and in the next instant her bra clasp was undone.

He touched her in the same reverent way he'd handled her pictures. The private, noncommercial ones she'd taken only for her pleasure. Except, he seemed to find as much pleasure in looking at them as she did. All the nervous nail biting had been for nothing.

She lay back against the cushions while he finished unbuttoning her blouse, and then she watched as he got rid of his shirt.

He nudged her with a light poke of his elbow. "Am I going to have to do all the work?"

"Sounds good to me."

He laughed. "Why did I bother asking?"

"No clue."

Prompted by him easing aside her bra cups and flicking his tongue over one of her nipples, she gave in and shoved the blouse sleeves off, letting the bra go with it.

He switched to the other nipple and then murmured. "I think we should go to the bedroom."

"Well, we did trash one of their couches already."

"I know. I got a bill for it."

She sat up straight, her eyes wide. "Oh, my God. Are you kidding?"

He grinned. "Yeah."

Gasping, she smacked him on the arm, but he caught her wrist with one hand and attacked the snap of her jeans with the other. He got her zipper down in a flash. But instead of doing the expected, he slid his hand between her thighs, against the denim, causing a pleasant friction that made her squirm.

"Bedroom," she whispered.

He got up first and helped her up, kissing her as she got to her feet. Not gentle kisses. The really deep kind that would land them back on the couch if she didn't force him to move. Which he did grudgingly, backward, as if he couldn't bear to break contact with her mouth.

When they both nearly stumbled over the end table, he sobered and led her the rest of the way. The bedroom drapes were drawn, thank goodness, because he already had his slacks halfway down and immediately stepped out of them. This time his boxers were black silk.

She'd had her jeans partway down, too, but they were tight and required more effort. Assistance he gladly rendered, going to one knee and tugging the denim over her thighs, kissing skin as he exposed it all the way down to her knees.

He didn't raise himself as she stepped out of the jeans, didn't try to pull off her panties, but planted a kiss against the silk as if it weren't there at all. That's how she felt, anyway. There might as well not have been a barrier. His heat was so intense it was as if he'd slipped his tongue between her folds.

With a startled cry, she realized he'd slid his finger under the elastic and had found the spot that drove her wild. She clutched his shoulders and tried to force him to his feet, but he insistently massaged, stroked, brought her close to the brink.

"Jack, no. Wait."

"Why?"

She moaned, trying to wiggle away from him, but his other hand held her derriere too firmly, and any movement merely created more unbearable friction.

With no choice in the matter, all she could do was give in to the pleasure. Sighing, she moved her legs a little farther apart, and that's when he slipped her panties down.

Naked and quivering, she felt his lips resume driving her insane, joined now with fingers from his other hand, slipping inside her.

He pumped, hard, as he flicked his wicked tongue until every muscle in her body was tightened like a bowstring. Finally, she cracked, coming so hard, he had to grab her around the hips before she fell.

Jack eased her onto the bed. She thought he was going to climb next to her, give her a chance to catch her breath, but instead he settled between her legs. Looking at her with glazed eyes, he put his hands beneath her legs and lifted them up until they rested on his shoulders.

When he scooted up, he grabbed one of the pillows from the head of the bed, pushed it under her hips.

"Oh," she said, still having aftershocks from her orgasm. He clearly intended to kill her with sex, which seemed like a fine idea.

He leaned over her until he hovered, his warm breath brushing her face, his eyes focused and fixed, and... What she saw there—

With no warning at all, he thrust into her, making her whole body spasm with the most intense pleasure she'd ever felt. He'd relit her climax, and she had to grab fistfuls of the comforter just to keep on the bed.

This was no slow tease, this was a full-out, rock-your-world, take-no-prisoners assault on her senses, on her body, on her sanity.

It was everything hot she'd ever dreamed of, and while she'd known Jack had a wildness to him, she'd never imagined this. Looking at him above her, as he took her for his own, claimed her with his cock and his eyes, it was a revelation. No one had ever looked at her like that, as if he'd wanted to brand her forever. Nothing had ever made her feel like this. The connection between them was much more than physical, and for the life of her, she didn't know what to do except submit.

She gasped for breath as he bent her nearly double, as he shook above her, as a drop of sweat from his brow dripped onto her cheek.

There was simply no way to close her eyes, despite the tremors coursing through her. She was held utterly by his ferocious gaze.

How could she reconcile the man on the television, always composed, always a gentleman, with this wild creature? He had no business letting himself be so tamed. He needed to be let free, to let this part of himself out of the small box, and not just with her. Not just with sex.

He was too big for the life he'd found himself in, and if there was anything she could give him before this was over, it was going to be to help him see that.

If she didn't die first.

Her mouth opened, but before she could speak, or even scream, his lips took hers, and devoured her, just as he devoured her sex.

He was groaning, low and raw and his power was so amazing, she could have come just from looking at him. But that wasn't his plan, either. He was going to make her come apart at the seams.

His thrusts became more erratic and, seconds later, he came. He hung there, over her, his arms stiff and trembling on either side of her, his breath heavy and his chest rising and falling as if he'd never be calm again.

Her legs were still over his shoulders; her hands still gripped the comforter. And in that moment she knew she wasn't going to get over this man. Ever.

SHE OPENED HER EYES to find Jack staring at her. His head propped up with one hand, he smiled, then brushed a lock of hair away from her face and tucked it behind her ear.

"You slept," he said softly.

"How long?"

"Just about half an hour."

"Did you sleep?"

He shook his head. "I have something to tell you."

A wave of panic hit her. He looked so damn serious. "If you don't want to see me anymore, it's okay." The words were barely out of her mouth and she wanted to kick herself. Not just because he looked so displeased. But because it sounded so pathetic, insecure.

He sighed. "That's the furthest thing from my mind." He paused, sighed again. "I wanted you to be the first to know that I probably won't be renewing my contract with the network."

She got up on one arm, hand bracing her head, to face him eye to eye. "Really? What are you going to do?"

"It's not for certain yet, but it's doubtful they'll meet my demands, and I'm prepared to walk." He looked down at the circles he was tracing on her naked hip.

"Are you sure you want to do that?"

"Yes. As sure as I've ever been."

"Look at me."

He met her gaze and gave her an indulgent smile.

"You're really sure."

"Yes," he said, unblinking.

"It's about field time, isn't it?" Her heart had already started to sink. Though his schedule was hectic here, as long as he was in New York she'd be able to see him.

He slowly nodded.

"Which means that you'll be out trotting around the globe," she said as cheerfully as she could muster. "That's wonderful, Jack. It's what you're supposed to do. You shouldn't be trapped into something so tame. You've got so much more to offer."

He abandoned her hip and covered her hand, squeezing gently, looking at her with such hopeful eyes. "I want you to come with me."

"What?" Her laugh came out a sad croak.

"I do the reporting. You take the pictures."

She didn't know what to say. She could only stare at him in stunned disbelief. "You don't even have another job yet." Suspicion stopped her cold. "Do you?"

"No, but it won't be hard to get one."

"For you, yes."

"We'll be a package deal." He sat up, excitement lighting his face. "Come on, Madison. We'd be so good together. I know it in my gut."

Her gaze traveled down his chest to his flat belly. The sheet obstructed further view but she didn't have to see to know what was there. "No fair asking me like this," she murmured, trying to stall for time. She couldn't process any of this.

He chuckled and leaned over to kiss her. She responded. How could she not? But her mind was a tornado of thoughts, swirling at reckless speed. They barely knew each other. She was a celebrity photographer and she took kids' portraits. Of course he didn't know that part. Thank God.

And just because he'd altered her very chromosomes when he'd made love to her, it still didn't mean that they were meant to be together.

She shook her head. "I can't believe your network would let you go that easily—not to work for the competition."

"I can't work as an anchor. Not for five years, according to my contract. So what? That's not what I want to do. You showed me that."

Her head started to hurt. Was this a dream? "How?"

"Your passion. Your drive. I used to be like you. Not anymore. I don't love my work. It's only a job now." He smiled wryly. "Yeah, it pays well, but it also comes at a high price."

She suddenly felt so weak she didn't think she could hold her head up any longer. She lay back against the pillows and stared at the ceiling.

"I realize this came out of nowhere. I just want you to think about it. Okay?"

She barely nodded. It seemed to require too much effort.

"You're too good to be chasing celebrities, Madison. You could be doing so much more." He touched her arm, stroked up and down. "You might be part of a package deal at the beginning, but you'll be earning your own way. Hell, after you get the cover—"

She laughed humorlessly. "I'm not going to get the cover."

He stopped stroking her arm. "What do you mean?"

She shrugged. "The competition is stiff. I mean, I took some good shots, but...I don't have my hopes up."

He studied her a long time. Too long. She regretted the admission.

"Have you shown them to anyone?"

"Not yet." She smiled. "I'll probably show them to Talia, an editor at *Today's Man,* and get her opinion. I still have time to change my mind and submit different shots than I've chosen."

He stayed silent a long time, probably wondering why she hadn't shown them to him. They were good. Just not great. "Why didn't the ones you showed me make the cut?" he asked.

She looked sharply at him. "You have to ask?"

He exhaled loudly and scrubbed at his face. "Use them, Madison. I don't care."

But he *did.* She knew it. Just like she'd known he'd be hitting the road.

"DO I GET A PREVIEW?" Talia asked Madison, looking at her over black-rimmed glasses.

She'd just walked into the editor's office. "May I take my coat off first?"

"You're not wearing one, although I can't fathom why. It's forty-eight degrees out there."

"I can't afford one. You guys don't pay me enough."

"Don't look at me." Talia took off her glasses and pinched the bridge of her nose. "They don't pay me enough, either. Let's see the pictures."

"Wouldn't that be a conflict of interest?" Madison kept a straight face.

"Don't be a twit. You know I'm not one of the judges." She held out her hand. "Let's see."

Madison set down the flat leather portfolio. Talia's eagerness surprised her. So did her presence, for that matter. Madison had really hoped to use her office in private. "I thought you had a meeting."

"It was pushed back to three-thirty." Talia frowned. "Are you trying to avoid me?"

"No, of course not. I just haven't decided on my final submission."

"The deadline is day after tomorrow."

"Gee, I didn't know that. Thanks."

Talia frowned and stiffened defensively. "What's wrong with you?"

Madison sank into a chair, so tired she could hardly stand. "I'm sorry. I am really, really sorry. You of all people don't deserve my sarcasm."

Talia's expression softened. "Apology accepted. What's going on?"

"I don't know." She knew. Too well. After all that hype, all that boasting about how the cover would be hers, she knew she'd failed. Not exactly failed. She actually had dozens of great shots that would have the judging staff drooling for a week. They wouldn't even be able to choose which one to put on the cover. But she couldn't use them.

And then there was Jack himself. And the huge question that had loomed over them the past three nights. He hadn't pushed for an answer and she hadn't volunteered one.

"Guess I'm just tired," she told Talia, who continued to watch her with a puzzled frown.

"Well, show me the photographs. I'll tell you how fabulous they are. How you're going to wipe the floor with the other submissions. That'll make you feel better."

"Right." Madison wanted to cry. She brought out the photos, but could barely look at Talia while she examined them. It was too painful to see the disappointment that was surely on her face.

17

JACK CHECKED HIS hair and teeth a final and unnecessary time before leaving his dressing room. This was just another interview, he reminded himself. No reason for the suddenly dry mouth as if he were a nervous rookie reporter.

For God's sake, he'd interviewed two presidential candidates, the president, the first lady, prime ministers, countless heads of states, in fact. Important people who had something significant to say. Madam Zora's interview was for entertainment purposes. Nothing more.

The stage had already been set, and thankfully the interview wouldn't begin live. They'd be introduced off camera and in place before the cameras started rolling, almost as if they'd been caught in midinterview.

He liked getting there before his guest arrived, but as soon as he got to the set he saw that she had already settled into the guest's chair, her large black satiny form seeming to absorb everything in the room.

It was an odd kind of energy he'd felt once before on an assignment in Haiti. A self-proclaimed medicine woman had practically stalked him, forewarning of bandits and ambushes. Frankly, she'd scared the hell out of him. Especially since one of her predictions had been on target and had forced them to turn around. Although in the area he'd been traveling, any warning wasn't a far stretch.

Madam Zora smiled up at him as he approached, her dark eyes warm and kind, and quite astonishingly, immediately put him at ease. Gleaming gold hoops weighed down her fleshy earlobes but that was the extent of her jewelry. She extended a bare well-manicured hand to him.

"Mr. Logan, I am honored."

"It's Jack." Their palms met and his tingled. A kind of prickly feeling you got after being shocked. He barely stopped himself from jerking back his hand. "Thank you for coming," he said, slowly releasing her and then claiming the seat across from her.

Behind them one of the producers gave direction to a stagehand while Sally from makeup hovered off to the side, but Madam Zora's gaze stayed eerily on Jack. Never wavering, not so much as a blink.

"Would you like some water or coffee?" he asked.

She shook her head. "Beverages have already been offered."

"Good." He glanced at the cue clock, and then at the stagehand, signaling for water. He rarely needed to keep a cup handy, but he had a feeling today he might need it. "We'll be going on the air in three minutes. Why don't you tell me a little about yourself?"

Her smile showed off perfectly even white teeth. "You already know about me."

"Of course I read the bio you provided—"

She started slowly shaking her head, a knowing smile dancing at the corners of her mouth. "We have a mutual acquaintance."

Madison. He didn't say anything at first. Only stared. Hoping she'd elaborate. Hoping she wouldn't. "I don't think so."

Madam Zora laughed softly. "She would not appreciate your denial. She is highly spirited, that one."

Jack drew in a breath. Of course the woman knew nothing about Madison. She could be talking about anyone. He knew lots of women. She was guessing. The comment was broad enough.

He gave her a smile he hoped didn't come off as patronizing. "How about you fill me in on how you became the popular Madam Zora?"

Her eyebrows went up. "I am here to talk about you. Not me."

He chuckled. "No, as a matter of fact, you're—" He stopped when he saw the gleam of determination in her eyes. This wasn't good. They needed a postponement. Needed time to set her straight. He waved for the stagehand, but Mike pointed to the cue clock. Twenty seconds and they'd be on the air.

She leaned forward with great effort to reach his hand, and then patted it, soothingly, bestowing that calm he'd felt upon first meeting her. "Don't worry," she whispered. "It will be good. It will all be good."

Jack froze. He almost missed his cue a second before they went live. He straightened, so did Madam Zora. Silently clearing his throat, he smiled. The one the public expected. Even though his insides were jumping.

"Today we have with us Madam Zora." He looked from the camera to her. "Some people refer to you as the psychic to the stars. Does that bother you?"

She settled back in her chair, her black satin caftan

making her seem to blend into the background. "I see things others don't. So they call me a psychic."

"When did you discover you had this gift?"

She smiled. "You are not a believer."

Damn. This was not supposed to happen. He was gonna kill his producer. "Actually, I haven't given the matter much thought."

"Ah, then perhaps I should convince you?"

He forced a smile. "I think I like asking the questions better."

"Yes, you do. And you will ask many. Important ones. All around the world." Madam Zora smiled kindly. "And she will be there with you, by your side."

Jack lost it. For the first time in his career, he was rendered speechless. He gave the signal to cut. And that's the last thing he remembered.

STILL REELING FROM his disastrous interview with Madam Zora, Jack sat in his office away from the morning crew's curious looks. Everyone probably thought he'd gone off the deep end. He wasn't sure he hadn't. The woman had gotten so damn close to the truth. How could she have known about Madison? About his decision to leave the show? It was crazy.

Jack leaned back in his chair and stared at his desk, littered with e-mails, reports from the news desk, faxes, some of his own research for tomorrow's show. On his walls were pictures of him and three different presidents, him sparring with his coanchor, Andrea Scott, whom he'd always called Andy, and an assortment of photos from the field.

On his credenza behind him stood one of his Emmys

and a parade of mementos given to him by several world leaders.

Outside his office, his staff rushed around trying to keep abreast of a breaking news story, a groundbreaking story that could reverse legislation on assisted suicide for the terminally ill.

If he said he wouldn't miss all this, he'd be a liar. There was comfort and a sense of community in being in the middle of this maelstrom. And undeniable safety. His ratings were outstanding, which gave him power and security and allowed him to call most of the shots. Unfortunately, the one that mattered the most to him was the deal breaker.

He'd know for sure by the end of the week, but he hadn't fooled himself. What good was a morning anchor who wouldn't be here forty percent of the time? He understood their position. But this was his life. He had one shot at living it the way he wanted to.

He'd even prepared his speech for Lana and Andy and his personal staff. They'd be shocked, horrified, disappointed. Hopefully, they'd also understand.

Madison was his biggest concern. That one night that had changed everything between them. He couldn't stop thinking about her. They'd spent nearly every night together since, the sex was fantastic, the familiarity that was growing even better, but she'd never talked about his proposal. When he brought it up, her foolish optimism that the network would cave in alarmed him. Her avoidance spoke volumes. What he couldn't figure out was whether she simply didn't want to leave New York or she thought she had a better future sticking with celebrity pictures.

Maybe she was just plain scared. One thing for certain was that she didn't appreciate her extraordinary talent. Following that logic, she probably doubted she could make it in a new area. Probably hadn't helped that he implied she'd make it on his coattails. He was wrong to have put it that way. He'd only wanted to offer her security while she got her feet wet.

If she got the cover, that could change everything. Problem was, she'd finally shown him the photos she'd selected to submit. They were good. Damn good. But he doubted any of them would end up on the cover. But he knew of one for certain that would.

He unlocked the second drawer where he kept personal items, and withdrew the set of photos she'd given him from her private stock. He looked at each of them, flinching twice at the intensely raw emotion she'd captured, particularly in one.

Damn, it was a dicey move.

She needed that cover. It would bring her the confidence she needed to follow him. He took a deep breath. Or it could just as easily send her in another direction. Either way, she deserved the cover.

He picked up the phone and called for his driver.

The ride over to the offices of *Today's Man* was short. He should've taken a cab. The job's perks, which he'd taken for granted and would admittedly miss, made him shake his head at himself. Gave him a shot of that damn uncertainty that occasionally plagued him.

He ignored it. He was human. Misgivings were inevitable. But deep down he knew he was right to quit. Knew he was right in what he was about to do.

With the envelope of photographs tucked firmly

under his arm, he stopped at the receptionist's desk, asked for directions to Talia's office and went to her door. It was open. She looked up and peered at him over black-rimmed glasses, her red lips forming a surprised *O*.

"Talia?"

She nodded, her eyes widening comically behind the thick glasses.

"I'm Jack Logan, a friend of Madison's, and I have a big favor to ask you," he said, and closed the door behind him.

MADISON HAD SMOKED one cigarette in her entire life. At sixteen. It had been awful. She had hated the taste, hated the smoke floating up to her face and making her eyes water. So why did she have the sudden urge to light up now?

Maybe a candy bar would calm her nerves? She fumbled inside her camera bag, until she gave up and dumped the contents out on the corner of Talia's desk.

The editor looked up from the article she was reviewing. "Gee, be my guest."

"Sorry." She found two mini-Butterfingers and offered one to Talia, who shook her head. Madison unwrapped one and stuffed it into her mouth, her gaze going to her watch. "They know I'm in here, right? They won't be calling my apartment. Of course they do have my cell number, too."

As if anyone would be calling her.

Madison closed her eyes. Why was she doing this to herself? The reason Gloria hadn't called was because Madison hadn't gotten the cover. She hadn't believed she would. Not really. But there'd been the tiniest seed of hope....

"Relax, damn it. You're making me nervous." Talia took off her glasses and rubbed her eyes, carefully, presumably so she wouldn't get all that black stuff she wore smudged. "You'll get the call. You've got the cover. It's a no-brainer."

Madison opened her eyes and stared suspiciously at Talia. She'd seen the photographs Madison had submitted, and although her reaction had been favorable, she hadn't exactly been blown away. "Do you know something I don't?"

"Me?" She blinked and then put her glasses back on and said blandly, "Sure," before promptly returning her attention to the article.

Madison slumped in her chair. She wished Jack were here. Better yet, she wished she were with him at his apartment. Snuggling together on the couch in front of the massive television that actually lowered from a nook in the ceiling with the touch of a single button.

She felt incredibly at home there. In just two short weeks she'd come to know his housekeeper, his driver, even the doorman. They were all great. They even helped run interference with the paparazzi vultures that sometimes camped outside his building.

She vaguely knew a couple of them, and never being without her camera bag, she got a kick out of the fact that they thought she was there for the same reason—to get an incriminating picture of Jack. Not someone they'd love to catch in the act.

At the same time it really bothered her to be associated with those bottom-feeders, with their unscrupulous methods and unrelenting determination to capture stars in the worst possible light. Granted, the press and media probably considered her only a couple of steps above the paparazzi. There was little prestige in being a celebrity photographer, unless you were at the very top, like Scavullo or Annie Leibovitz, but at least it was honest work.

She couldn't help but think about Jack's offer, though, to get involved with serious, mainstream journalism. Not that she thought anything would come of it. It was just a fantasy she indulged in when she was stuck taking pictures of squirming kids. The network wouldn't let him go. Not with his popularity being at its peak. They'd compromise.

Probably not entirely to Jack's liking, but he could be persuaded. He loved his creature comforts, like getting reservations whenever he wanted, enjoyed the power of his position at the network.

The phone rang and she nearly fell out of the chair. So startled she couldn't immediately figure out which phone it was. It was Talia's. Her editor answered it and then, grinning, held the phone out to Madison.

"I GOT IT," she said as soon as Jack answered his phone.

"Congratulations, baby." Of course, he knew exactly what she was talking about. "We're celebrating tonight. Anywhere you want to go. How does San Francisco sound?"

"We can't tonight. You have that late meeting, remember?"

"I'll cancel."

"No, you won't. We'll go out tomorrow." She giggled

like a schoolgirl and swung her legs up onto Talia's desk. Bless her, she'd gone down to the lobby sundry store supposedly for a pack of gum. Madison knew better, and appreciated the privacy. "I still can't believe it."

"Why not? You're very good...wouldn't believe it when I told you, though." He paused. "Did they say which picture they're using?"

"Nope. And I didn't ask." She laughed. "I should have, I suppose. I was too shocked. Anyway, guess I'll find out later this afternoon. I have a meeting with the head honcho." She paused for dramatic effect. "To discuss my new staff position."

The silence lasted too long.

"Jack?"

"Uh, yeah."

"Sorry, did I catch you at a busy time?"

"No, I, um..." He sighed into the phone. "Frankly, I was hoping you were giving some thought to my proposition."

She shrank at his softly spoken words. "Jack, you don't seriously think they'll let you go."

"They won't have a choice if they don't meet my terms." He let silence lapse once more. "Weren't you listening to me?"

"Of course I was." She rubbed the residual day's tension at the back of her neck. This was her big shot. To be on staff at *Today's Man* was huge. She couldn't leave now. He didn't understand. He'd had his glory. Been at the top. She was just clawing her way up now.

"I'm being summoned by my secretary," he said. "Can I call you later?"

"Sure."

"Tell you what. You're going to be busy. You call me."

"Busier than you?" She chuckled at the small absurdity.

That dreaded silence again. "I'm proud of you, baby," he whispered before he hung up.

She sat there, feeling a little deflated. Not that it was his fault. He didn't understand. At one time he would have, but it'd been so long since he'd had to struggle that he'd forgotten what it was like to have to accept every crumb in the hope that someday someone would screw up and drop a whole biscuit in your lap.

Besides, she'd seen the uncertainty in his eyes. He didn't want to give up what he had going for him. If the network didn't cave, he'd compromise. She hoped.

No, she didn't. What was she thinking? He wanted to be out in the field. That was his passion. Still, couldn't he do both? Damn it, she wanted him here. In Manhattan with her.

It was all way too much to think about.

IT FELT WEIRD not wearing jeans, but Madison had run out and splurged on a pair of real honest-to-goodness slacks to meet with Gloria Armstrong. She shouldn't consider it a splurge. Although she and Jack stayed in a lot, eventually she'd have to pay more attention to the rags hanging in her closet.

A steady paycheck was sure going to help. She cleared her throat, started to drag her clammy palms down her thighs and remembered she wasn't wearing jeans. She made loose fists and blew into each of them and then knocked on Gloria's door.

"Come in." The older woman came from around her

desk, her hand outstretched. "Please forgive me if we've met before, Madison."

She smiled. "No, we haven't, Ms. Armstrong." Madison had only seen her in the halls. Hard to miss all that beautiful white hair styled in a perfect French twist.

"Please sit. And call me Gloria." She went around her desk and reclaimed her black leather power chair with its high, cushioned back. "Congratulations, by the way. Brava. Your photographs are outstanding."

"Thank you."

"Frankly, I don't know how you managed to get them." The woman's blue eyes twinkled with amused suspicion. "Mr. Logan has always been quite elusive."

"He was very difficult at first," she said slowly, not sure if there was an implication she'd missed. "But then we came to an understanding."

"Well, whatever magic you worked to get these—" she flattened her manicured hands on a large white envelope "—we sure could use on a permanent basis."

Madison stared at the envelope. Had she missed something everyone else saw? She heard Gloria talking but couldn't focus on what she was saying.

"I'm sorry," she said to the older woman. "You were saying?"

Gloria frowned. "We were discussing salary?"

She nodded, trying to remember what the pictures looked like. It had only been a week since she submitted them, and she had copies, but she couldn't for the life of her remember. "May I see those?"

Gloria's frown deepened before she glanced down at the envelope and picked it up.

"I'm sorry," Madison said earnestly, as she put out

her hand. God, she didn't want to blow the job, but she had to have another look. Now. Not later. A weird feeling in her belly told her something was wrong.

She took the envelope and opened it like a starving man given his first meal in a week. She fumbled and almost dropped the photographs when she saw the first one. The one marked Cover.

Gloria said something but Madison couldn't hear her. She just stared, wordless with shock.

IT WAS NEARLY MIDNIGHT before she got ahold of him. But as soon as he answered the phone, Madison asked, "Why, Jack?"

He sighed. "Talia isn't to—"

"I already know how." Laying across her bed, she rubbed her temple in a round soothing motion. Only she didn't feel soothed. "I wanna know why."

"For the cover."

She sucked in a breath. Too tired, too emotional, she should have waited until morning. Too late. "You shouldn't have interfered."

He didn't say anything for a long moment. "You're right. But do I get points for my motive being pure?"

She was too cranky to let him off easy. "You didn't want me to use those photographs. And don't deny it."

"No, but I wanted you to get the cover more."

Why did he have to say all the right things? The fact remained that he had no business getting in her business. Yes, he was powerful. Yes, in a way he'd branded her as his, but that didn't give him the right to—

But he did understand. He did remember how important it was to catch that biscuit. He'd proven it.

"What's wrong, Madison? Are you mad because now you have to make a choice?"

"I'm not mad." She yawned. He sounded tired, too. "What choice?"

"To stay here where you're safe, no more risks to take. Or to go with me."

"Okay, now I'm mad."

He chuckled.

"Go to sleep, Jack. Sounds like we both need it." She hung up and then realized she hadn't asked about his meeting.

TODAY WAS NOT GOING to be fun. Not only did she have to kiss and make up with Jack once he was done at the studio, but she had to give Shelly her notice. After her stupid panic attack yesterday, she'd made nice with Gloria, they'd come to terms financially, and Madison couldn't have been more thrilled. But, man, did she hate having to bail on Shelly.

Madison had decided to offer her time on Sundays for as long as Shelly needed her, but she knew Shelly was still going to be unhappy. Though Madison didn't have a choice.

Choice.

The word still rankled her as she pulled open the door to Shelly's Family Portraits. What choice did getting the cover give her? Taking that particular picture of him, sans shirt, staring at her as if he wanted to devour her did not exactly prove her a great photographer. Hell, that had probably been the easiest photo she'd ever taken. All thanks to him.

Still, she appreciated the boost it gave. But when

the day was done, she was now a celebrity photographer full-time who made more money and earned more respect. Which was good enough for her.

Besides, he wasn't going anywhere.

"You are in big trouble." Shelly planted her hands on her hips and narrowed her gaze in accusation before the door had even closed behind Madison.

No way could she have already heard about *Today's Man's* offer. It just wasn't possible. "Why?" she asked slowly.

"You could have told me about Jack Logan."

"Told you what about him?"

Shelly looked genuinely ticked. "I had to hear it on the afternoon news."

"Hear what?"

"That he's leaving his spot on the show."

Madison stared, her mouth open. Her heart started to pound. "You heard this on the news."

"Yeah, about an hour ago." Shelly frowned. "Are you okay?"

"No," She swallowed and started backing up. "No, I'm not. I have to go, Shelly. I'll call, okay?"

"Wait!"

She didn't. She stepped out into the street, stuck two fingers in her mouth and whistled for all she was worth. The approaching cab stopped abruptly, probably because of her waving arm, since it was cold and his windows were up. She got in, gave him Jack's address and then got out her phone on the slim chance he was still at the studio.

No luck. Her phone was dead. She should have charged it last night. But she hadn't, and now she just hoped that Jack was at home.

They got to his building in great time, and as she paid the cabbie the uniformed doorman saw her and hurried to open her door. She got out, a little breathless. Probably nerves.

Across the street the paparazzi had already camped out. At least a dozen of them, arguing with cops over illegal parking spots.

"Hey, Manny, is he home?"

The older man closed the cab door and shook his head. The sadness in his eyes gave her a chill. "He just left. For the airport."

The ground seemed to shift beneath her feet. "The what?"

He nodded. "La Guardia. About twenty minutes ago."

She turned to see if she could still catch the cab that had dropped her off. Too late. She stuck out her arm to hail another one. "Do you know what airline?"

He shrugged and waved to another cab. He named two possibilities. "Try the major ones first, but I'm not sure."

"Thanks, Manny."

He smiled, nodded and opened the cab door.

She alternately cussed and prayed all the way to the airport. The ride was too damn long and gave her way too much time to think. To sink deeper into depression. He'd actually left the network. Had he known last night? Of course he had. That's probably what his meeting had been about. But she'd been too wrapped up in her own world to have even asked.

They arrived at La Guardia in record time, and she added forty to the fare as she'd promised. The first airline she'd thought of had turned out to be a dud. She ran to the second one, her head bobbing as she scanned the crowded thoroughfare.

She didn't see him, but she saw the microphones and cameras about a hundred yards away. She rushed closer and then she saw him. Looking tired, annoyed, disgusted as he tried to dodge the media.

"Jack!"

He didn't hear her so she climbed up on the only vacant chair along a row of waiting travelers. She cupped her hands around her mouth and called his name again. He apparently heard but didn't spot her until she frantically waved her arms.

He smiled. A big warm smile that made her stumble when she tried to get down. None too happy about it, a paunchy middle-aged man kept her from falling on her rear.

She murmured her thanks and hurried toward Jack. Ignoring the crowd around him, he rushed to meet her halfway.

"God, I'm glad to see you." He kissed her long and hard, oblivious to the excited buzz and camera flashes. "I didn't know if you'd gotten my message."

"I didn't."

"I left a voice mail on your cell."

"My phone's dead." She sniffed. Of all the stupid things, she felt like crying.

Someone stuck a microphone under his nose. "Come on, Jack. Tell us why the hasty exit from—"

"Who's the woman?"

"Does she have anything to do with your leaving?"

He took her arm and pulled her alongside him. "The first-class lounge is right here. These guys can't get in."

The attendant recognized him and promptly welcomed them inside. Only three other people sat sipping drinks and watching television. They didn't even glance over.

Jack steered her toward a private, corner table and after she was seated, pulled his chair close to hers and took her hand. "If you didn't get my message, how did you know where to find me?"

"I went to your apartment. Manny told me. After I heard the news."

"What news?"

"About you."

He smiled and squeezed her hand. "It wasn't news to you. I told you first."

"Yeah, but I didn't think everything would happen so quickly, or that you'd—" She looked down at their joined hands.

"Or that I'd really do it?"

She nodded miserably.

"That's okay. Larry didn't believe me, either, and he's known me for a long time." He nudged her chin up. "Hey, cheer up."

"Cheer up?" She scowled at him. "You're leaving."

"Just for a few days. The whole thing leaked too soon, and the network president wanted to avoid as much publicity as possible. He's being decent about my resignation, so I figured a few days in Bermuda wouldn't hurt." Jack thought he saw her eyes start to well up, and his chest tightened. "Did you think I was just cutting out for good?"

She shrugged without looking at him. "I didn't know what to think. Everything happened so fast." Her sad eyes met his. "I just knew I didn't want you to leave without me."

"Good." He leaned over, hugged her and kissed the top of her hair, loath to let her go. "In my message I explained that I was leaving an open ticket for you."

She smiled against his chest. "Really?"

He nodded, held her closer. "I want you with me. Always. But whatever you decide, we'll work it out."

She pulled back to look at him. "I did know you would quit. That you should. In fact, I think I knew it before you did. But I guess I tricked myself into believing…"

"That I wouldn't go?"

She nodded. "I couldn't think about letting you go. I couldn't." The way she looked at him told him as much as her words. "So much has happened in such a short time. You, me. The cover, my new job, you quitting. My head's spinning with it all."

"You don't have to decide anything right now. We'll get away, think about things. Talk it out. The only thing I know for sure is that I care about you. I want you to be happy."

"Funny. The only thing I'm sure about is that I want you."

"Well then, that's easy. Because I'm a sure thing."

She stared at him for a long time. Then she leaned in and kissed him gently, hopefully, but too quickly.

"What?" he asked, as she shook her head.

"I think I owe Madame Zora an apology."

"She'll have to wait. Everything will have to wait."

Madison sighed, caressed his cheek with the back of her hand. "You're right. It's all about the passion."

Epilogue

"DOES EVERYONE HAVE champagne?" Gloria Armstrong looked around the large conference room, packed with other *Today's Man* staffers.

Madison turned to Jack and smiled. He winked and slid an arm around her shoulder. It was silly really, that he'd come for the party, especially since he'd had to travel for two days and nights to get here. But he'd insisted and she was absurdly glad he had after all.

Gloria, of course, knew about Madison leaving. She'd been honest with the woman from the beginning. Talia was the only other person who knew. Madison simply felt she owed her a heads-up, but the others had no clue and it wasn't going to be easy saying goodbye. The entire staff had been supportive and helpful and after only a few weeks of being part of their family, Madison was going to really miss the camaraderie.

"All right everyone, squeeze in." Gloria motioned with her free hand. "Get your glasses ready. And by the way, you can blame Madison for it being so crowded because she wanted this gathering to be in the office instead of the Waldorf."

After a round of good-natured boos, Gloria raised her glass.

Madison clutched Jack's arm. This was going to be so hard.

"You haven't changed your mind, have you?" he whispered.

"Yeah, right." She wanted to kiss him. Right now. The heck with everyone. "Do you have any idea how much I've missed you?"

"Ah, yes, as a matter of fact. It gets mighty cold in Afghanistan this time of year."

"So you just want me for my body?"

"Can I get back to you on that? Gloria's trying to get your attention."

After a well-placed elbow to his ribs, Madison turned back to her boss—technically the relationship would be in place for the next half hour anyway.

Gloria cleared her throat. Everyone quieted. "Here's to Madison and her cover on the highest-selling issue to date."

"Bravas" erupted. A couple of whistles and hoots and then everyone quieted while they sipped their champagne. When they started in again, Gloria held up her hand for silence.

"That was the good news, folks," she said, and the room grew impossibly quieter. "This is also a goodbye party."

The murmuring started. Some of the women from accounting and the art department looked directly at Madison. She smiled weakly.

"No, you're not getting rid of *me*," Gloria joked, and then looked somberly at Madison. "It seems our newest staff member has gotten a better offer."

All eyes went to Jack. He shrugged, looking a tad sheepish.

Madison laughed and slid an arm around his waist. "You haven't changed your mind, have you?"

He turned to face her, and tilted her chin up. The desire in his eyes made her knees weak. "Not a chance," he whispered and kissed her until the catcalls faded.

* * * * *

*Get ready to check in to the Hush Hotel
in April 2007 with*
Room Service *by Jill Shalvis.*

Here's a sneak preview…

Room Service
by
Jill Shalvis

A MAN STEPPED INTO the elevator. He wore black Levi's and battered boots, and a black long-sleeve shirt with the pink HUSH logo on his pec. His eyes were covered with mirrored aviator sunglasses, and when he shoved them to the top of his head and looked at Em, her heart stopped. Not because he was drop-dead gorgeous—no that description felt too neat, too pat, too…*GQ*. In fact, he was the furthest thing from *GQ* as she'd ever seen.

He was tall, probably six-four, all tough and rangy and hard-muscled. His hair was cropped extremely short, and was as dark as his fathomless eyes, set in a face that could encourage the iciest of women to ache. And in that face she saw a full life, as if he'd lived every single one of his years as fast and hard as he could.

Which wasn't to say he wasn't appealing. In truth, she couldn't tear her eyes off him. But she could tell he was the kind of man who would worry a mother, the kind of man a father sat on his porch holding a shotgun for. He seemed…street, tough as nails, edgy, possibly even dangerous.

And then he smiled.

Yeah, big and rough, and most definitely badass. This was a man who'd seen and done things, the sort of man who could walk through a brawl, give as good as he got and come out unscathed.

A warrior.

Em would have sworn her heart gave one last little flutter before it stopped altogether.

But the most surprising thing was what he said.

"Good, you're here."

Um…what? *Her?* Em looked behind her, but they were alone. *Me?* she mouthed, pointing to herself, nearly swallowing her tongue when he nodded.

"You." His voice wasn't hard and cold, as she might have expected, but quiet and deep and tinged with a hint of the south, which only added to the ache in her belly.

What was it about a man with a hint of a slow, southern drawl?

Before she could process that thought—or any thought at all, actually—he slipped an arm around her, turning to smile at the two women who followed him onto the elevator. "See?" he said to them. "Here she is."

Both women were very New York, sleek and stunning, and…*laughing?* Whatever the man had said "see" to, they weren't buying it. "Come on, Chef," one said, shaking her head.

Em stood there, not quite in shock, but not quite in charge of her faculties either, because the man had her snug to his body, which she could feel was solid muscle, not an inch of excess, and warm, so very warm. Her head fit perfectly in the crook of his shoulder. At five-nine, she'd never fit into the crook of anyone's shoulder before—not a single one of the toads she'd dated—and the feeling of being…dare she think it?…petite and delicate…made her want to sigh. The feminist in her tried to revolt, but she was overcome by her secret princess.

Then the man holding her tipped his face to hers. He had a day's growth of dark stubble along his jaw, a silver stud in one ear, and the darkest, thickest eyelashes she'd ever seen. He could probably convince a nun to sin with one crook of a finger, Em thought dazedly.

He was still smiling, only it wasn't a sweet, fuzzy smile but a purely mischievous, trouble-filled one.

Gee, Grandma, how many teeth do you have? Really, she needed to get herself together. But he was so yummy she hadn't yet decided whether to smack him or grab him when he suddenly leaned in, brushing that slightly rough jaw to her ear, the friction of his day's growth to her soft skin making her shiver.

"Do you mind?" he whispered against her, his voice low and husky. "If I kiss you?"

Kiss her? She wanted to have his firstborn!

"Just for show," he murmured, hitching his head back to the other two women, drawing her in closer as if she'd already agreed.

Em's mind raced. He didn't look like the toads she'd been with lately. He didn't feel like a toad. But would she ever really know unless she kissed him?

No, it was crazy, it was beyond crazy, letting a perfect stranger touch her, much less *kiss* her, but something about his mocha eyes, about what she saw in them, which was places and experiences she'd never even dreamed about, made her let out a slow, if unsure, nod.

He rewarded her with a smile that finally met those eyes of his, and then lowered his mouth.

The two women behind them, the ones who'd been

laughing at him only a moment ago, both let out shocked gasps.

That was all Em heard before her mind shut itself off and became a simple recipient of sensations. His lips were firm yet soft, his breath warm and delicious, and on top of it all, the man smelled so good she could have inhaled him all day long.

As a result, her lips seemed to part by themselves, and at the unmistakable invitation, her prince let out a rough sound of surprise and deepened the kiss, his fingers massaging the back of her head at her nape, his other hand sliding down, down, *down,* coming to rest low on her spine, his fingers almost on her butt, anchoring her to him.

Oh my.

And the kiss…it didn't make any sense. She didn't know him from Adam, but somehow she felt as if that weren't really true, as if maybe she'd always known him, as if her body recognized the connection even if her brain couldn't place him. Confusing, bewildering, but she held onto him as if it didn't matter, and he kept kissing her, kissing her until she felt hot everywhere, until she was making little sounds in the back of her throat that would have horrified her if she could put together a single thought.

It was as if he knew the secret rhythm to which her body responded. As if they were made for each other. As if they were past lovers reuniting.

And yet it wasn't real. Logically Em knew this, even through the sensual, earthy haze he'd created, but it also seemed shockingly profound, and nothing, nothing at all like a simple toad's kiss.

Then he lifted his head, her perfect stranger, and for one beat in time looked every bit as flummoxed as she.

But the beat passed and he smiled—the smile being sin personified—and even her goose bumps got goose bumps.

She tried to respond in kind, she really did, but all she managed to do was to open her mouth, and quite possibly drool.

With one last stroke of his hand up her spine, a touch that somehow conveyed a carefully restrained passion and control, he pulled his arm free, and when the elevator doors opened, he pushed his gaping friends off the elevator.

Then he turned back to Em.

She stood there blinking like an owl, unable to switch her tongue from drool-mode to talk-mode.

"Thank you," he said.

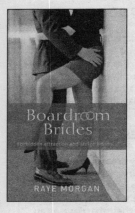

FREE!

2 Books
and a surprise gift!

We would like to take this opportunity to thank you for reading this Mills & Boon® book by offering you the chance to take TWO more specially selected titles from the Blaze™ series absolutely FREE! We're also making this offer to introduce you to the benefits of the Mills & Boon® Reader Service™—

- ★ FREE home delivery
- ★ FREE gifts and competitions
- ★ FREE monthly Newsletter
- ★ Exclusive Reader Service offers
- ★ Books available before they're in the shops

Accepting these FREE books and gift places you under no obligation to buy, you may cancel at any time, even after receiving your free shipment. Simply complete your details below and return the entire page to the address below. You don't even need a stamp!

YES! Please send me 2 free Blaze books and a surprise gift. I understand that unless you hear from me, I will receive 4 superb new titles every month for just £3.10 each, postage and packing free. I am under no obligation to purchase any books and may cancel my subscription at any time. The free books and gift will be mine to keep in any case.

K7ZEF

Ms/Mrs/Miss/Mr ....Initials ....
BLOCK CAPITALS PLEASE
Surname ....
Address ....

....
....Postcode ....

Send this whole page to:
UK: FREEPOST CN8I, Croydon, CR9 3WZ